Secrets Revealed

The Adventures of Silver Dove, Book Twelve

Eliza Scalia

Cover Illustration by: Katherine Lauren
Based upon the characters originally
designed by Suji Gallianetti and the further
work by Wayne F. Shurtz and Cheyanne and Jean
Buffkin

Dedicated to Alyssa Kronenberg who is helping me edit and do research for my next book series. Silver Dove has been a delight to write, but she has only been the beginning for me.

Chapter One
Colomba-
A New Hope

The warmth from the sun sinks into my skin, giving me a joyful feeling as the world seems to radiate happiness. This warmth is a welcome change from the freezing weather my area of Drew's Hollow has experienced recently. It feels like the entire world is thawing at the moment, and everyone around me seems to be feeling it too, since all around me I see happy faces, chatting and joking with those around them. It's almost funny how the weather seems to be mimicking my mood. When it was cold outside, I was nervous and terrified about everything that was going on with the Crow and all the other crazy stuff in my life. Now that it is so beautiful outside, I feel hopeful and more at peace. Everything feels like it will get better now and all these problems I've had for years now will go away. My little war may soon be over.

A few days ago, the Crow told me that he will stop his little crusade and that he will try to be better from now on. He said that he didn't want to hurt anyone anymore, at least he said that he didn't want to hurt me anymore. It might not be as good as not hurting everyone, but I'll take what I can get, I can't really expect too much from the guy. He has acted like a holy terror since the moment he arrived in my life, having him promise me this is almost a miracle, and I am very happy that it has happened.

Problem with believing the Crow though is that he might be lying to me. If I'm being really honest with myself, he's most likely lying to me, but I have to have some hope with this. If the Crow says that he is going to stop, then I have to feel some hope or else I'm just going to go nuts after all the craziness I have had to deal with. Hope is what's keeping me going at the moment. I don't know why, but everyone around me seems like everyone else is in a good mood as well for some reason, maybe they are enjoying the nice weather too.

Nat, Luis, and I head inside the school, leaving the warmth of the sun behind to be in the cold of the air conditioning. As we chat about random things, we pass by a poster hanging on the wall and Luis points at it as he speaks.

"Oh hey, the junior prom is coming up, are you guys going?" Well, I guess that explains why everyone around me seems excited and happy, they are all looking forward to this. With everything going on recently, I had completely forgotten about it. Luis had asked both Nat and I this question, but he looked at me as he asked this. Why is he looking at me? Is something going on that I don't know about? Nat just shrugs beside me.

"I'm going to go, but I don't have a date. I'll

still have a good time though." I nod my head, thinking of the couple of guys who have asked me to go with them, but I turned them all down. I can't really accept any of them if I don't have feelings for them, it would just be cruel. I did feel bad when they looked sad when I rejected them, one even cried, but I won't lie to them about how I feel. I look back at Luis who is looking at me excitedly, as if he really wants to say something. What is going on with him today?

"I'll be going too, but I don't have anyone to go with either. I will still have fun though because I'll have you guys." Luis clears his throat awkwardly, looking away as I see a faint blush forming on his cheeks. Is he embarrassed about something? Seriously, what is going on with him today? Is he about to prank me or something?

"So nobody has asked you to go with them?" This time I feel my cheeks growing warm in my embarrassment.

"Well a few people have asked me, but I said no. I wasn't really interested in them, and I couldn't just pretend that I am. I would want to go with someone I care about, not just anybody who asked me." I am looking down at my feet, but from the corner of my eye I can see Luis looking over at me awkwardly. Did I say something to make him feel uncomfortable?

"Well, Colomba, do you think that… maybe-you know, that you would-" Luis doesn't get to finish his question since he stops speaking, an angered look coming over my face. Before I can ask him what's wrong, I get my answer as I feel a strong arm wrap around my shoulders, pulling me in close to someone. Looking at the owner of the arm, I'm not surprised to see Alex with his usual smug, flirty grin on his face as he looks down at me like he is a lion, and I am his prey. My calm, happy morning has suddenly become a bit darker as I glare up at him.

"What do you want Alex?" I know that my voice sounds cold and not very friendly, but at this point I am just done with Alex. I am just done with dealing with this guy. He has hurt my friend Luis for far too long, he seems to mess with everyone he doesn't like, and hasn't taken no for an answer whenever he asks me out and this has been going on for three years! I'm tired of all this. Alex seems a bit surprised by my tone too since his eyes grow wide for a moment in shock before he gets his flirty face back in order. My gosh, this guy really can't take a hint.

"Hey Colomba, I know this is a bit last minute, and I know that things have been a bit tense between us for a while, but I was hoping that you could come with me to the dance this Friday and-" Alex pulls a bouquet of roses out from behind him and puts them right in front of my face. The anger inside me doubles in an instant as I push the flowers away from me and walk out of his grip.

"Oh, I am not dealing with this again!" I keep walking down the hall, already feeling my eyes water and my nose starts to sniffle as I hear Luis say something to Alex like he is scolding a stupid little kid.

"Didn't you learn your lesson when you asked

her out on Valentine's Day! She is allergic to roses you idiot! If you really liked her you would remember that!" I hear someone's feet running up behind me, and it only takes a moment for Luis to catch up and start walking beside me, pulling out some tissues from his backpack.

"You okay Colomba?" I smile gratefully as I take the tissues he offers me.

"Thanks Luis, and yeah I'm fine. You're right though, you would think that if he is really interested in a girl, then he would remember what she is allergic to at least." Luis chuckles at that, but still looks a bit upset by what just happened. I rest my hand on his shoulder, trying to help him calm down a bit. "Don't worry about me Luis, I'm fine. I just need to keep ignoring him until after the prom is over, then he'll stop. At least I hope he will." This statement only makes Luis look even more annoyed.

"This sucks that you have to wait for him to stop. I hate that he is always doing stuff like this to you. You deserve better than this. It sucks that you have to just live with him acting like this to you all the time." I give his shoulder a little squeeze, trying to hide my own annoyance, knowing that Luis is right about that.

"Yeah, but I can't control him, I can only control me. I've got to get to class, I have a test in first period, so I want to get there early. I'll see you later Luis." I walk away from him, not really wanting to let him go yet, but I don't want to upset him more. I'll see him later, so hopefully he will have calmed down by then. For now though, I don't want to let what just happened with Alex ruin my good mood. Things are changing, and I'm not going to lose hope that things will get better at this school because of Alex being his usual jerk of a self. I just need to keep believing that everything will soon be alright, and I will no longer need to worry about the Crow.

Chapter Two
Luis-
A New Plan

I watch Colomba leave me to walk towards her first class, still sniffling from the roses Alex tried to give her. What a miserable way to start the day. I swear, sometimes I want to just transform into the Crow and send my shadow dogs after Alex when I see him do stuff like this. After everything he has put Colomba and I through, he would deserve it. I can't let myself get distracted though by someone as pointless as him, I have a mission to complete.

A few days ago, I told Colomba (as the Crow) that I was going to stop with my mission, but I didn't tell her how. If I had been honest about that then she would not have been happy with me. I didn't lie to her, I just didn't tell her all the details. I will get rid of Silver Dove by finding out her secret identity. If I know who she really is, then I will have power over her, and she will actually listen to me. I can either expose her identity to the world, or she can follow my lead, it will be her choice. Shadow was not happy hearing about this plan, but she knows that she can't control me, nobody can. She may be the guardian of the medal, but I am the one wearing it. To reveal her true identity, I just need to make her powers fade during our regular fights. When Shadow first gave me the medal, she said there are only a few ways of doing that, and the easiest one would be too just make her exhausted. I just need to transform someone and have them wear her down, which shouldn't be too hard at all. I just need to find one more person to change and everything will finally start going my way. I can't believe it took me this long to figure out a plan like this. Oh well, I've thought of it now, and I'm going to make this work. It's got to work. With how bad the bullying is at my school; it probably won't take me long to find someone worthy of getting powers to combat Silver Dove. With how things are here, I can probably find someone by the end of the day.

I make it to my next class without any issues. Honestly, with how angry Alex looked a minute ago when I called him out, I'm a bit surprised he didn't try to get me as soon as Colomba was out of the picture. In the past, whenever I did something against him, he would beat me up as soon as he could without getting caught. Strange he didn't do that now. Oh well, it's not like I'm going to complain about not getting beat up. As soon as I think about that though, I overhear something that is worthy of being complained about.

At one of the desks close to me, someone is showing their friend the news broadcast on their phone, and it was easy to hear them say my name, the Crow.

"Although investigations have been occurring

since the Crow and Silver Dove first appeared," the voice of the news broadcaster says in their annoying, nasally voice, "there seem to be no results in figuring out their secret identities. Silver Dove seems to be keeping her promise of keeping our community safe, while the Crow is also keeping his promises to try and harm us." I feel my hands clench into fists when I hear her say that. I promised to punish those who deserve it and protect the weak. I didn't promise what you said you lying cow. "Despite that promise though, the Crow has not won a single battle with Silver Dove, not one. Makes you wonder how many more failures it will take for the Crow to finally realize he is never going to win against our champion, Silver Dove."

I put headphones in my ears and play some music, trying desperately to drown out the sound of the news. How dare she speak about me like that!? Doesn't she know who I am and what I'm capable of?! She wouldn't be laughing at me if I focused my attention on wherever she is. I'll need to remember this when I get Silver Dove out of my way. There will be a lot of people who will need to learn their lesson once I take power. Alex will be at the top of that list though. He will need to suffer for all that he has done to me and everyone else in this school. More importantly though, he needs to suffer for what he has done to Colomba. He has put her through far too much to not get punished. Angella will also be near the top of the list for how cruel she is towards everyone, even towards Colomba a few times. They all need to learn that they should never hurt Colomba.

Thankfully, I don't have to wait long for class to start and the people beside me to put away their phone. Pulling out my headphones and putting them away, I try my best to pay attention, but my mind is still stuck on what the news said about me. They have a lot to learn about me and my purpose here. I'm sure I will be a good teacher to them, I will admit though that I won't be the kindest teacher.

Well at least they won't have to wait long to finally see me beat Silver Dove. It will happen, I know it. I just need to find one last soldier to do exactly what I say.

Chapter Three
Colomba-
Kaley

A few class periods have passed since my little run in with Alex this morning, and thankfully I haven't seen him again since then. Right now I'm in English class, a class I get to share with Luis and Nat. We are all silently reading from the latest book the teacher is having us read. It's honestly a pretty boring book, and I would rather be doing anything else right now. I mean I love to read, I could read practically anything, and I hate this boring, stupid waste of paper. Why do all the books we have to read for English class have to be either boring or really depressing? There usually isn't an in between for this, they are usually awful and make you want to hate everything. Right now, what I hate more than anything though is this book.

As we all calmly read the book, probably all of us are hating this thing at the moment, a harsh sound interrupts us. Looking behind me, I'm not surprised to see Angela laughing coldly at a piece of paper in her hands. She is looking at the paper as if she is reading the funniest thing she has seen in ages. Beside her, a girl I know in passing by the name of Kaley, is blushing like crazy seeing Angela reading the paper.

"I told you that you needed to pass the note, not read it." Kaley almost growls these words at Angela in her anger. Her anger only makes Angela laugh even harder, like the cold little witch she is.

"Trust me freak, you don't want them to read this. They would laugh at you too." She breaks off laughing again as the entire class watches them in confusion.

"How could a girl like you have a crush on them?" Angela waves her hand over to her side, towards Luis and Nat beside her. Wait, does Kaley have a crush on Luis? Is that what all this is about? What's so wrong about liking Luis? He's a super amazing guy. To a girl like Angella though, she probably views him as unworthy of her attention. Only a prince would be worthy of the princess she thinks she is. "You must be a serious freak to want to go out with them!" Kaley looks so crushed when Angela calls them a freak. Before anybody can do anything, the bell signaling the end of class goes off, and Kaley runs out of the room, tears starting to stream down her face. I feel my face growing warm as anger rises in my heart.

"Why did you do that Angela?! Don't you have any decency at all?!" Angela turns to look at me as if I am being a complete idiot.

"C'mon Colomba, anybody like her deserves to be laughed at, I mean she's a complete freak." What does she mean by "anybody like her"? That doesn't matter, what matters is that I'm upset with Angela.

"That doesn't mean anything Angela, just because you feel some way about a person doesn't mean that you treat them like trash! And who cares if she likes someone?! Why does that even matter?!" I take in a deep breath, calming myself down when I realize that practically the entire class is looking at the two of us in shock, almost like they expect a full-on fight to break out. Shaking my head, I walk away from her. "You're so pathetic." I growl at her as I leave the room. Behind me, I can hear Angela screaming at me, calling me all sorts of terrible things, saying that I'm the pathetic one, not her. Funny part is though that she is saying this to all the people that remain in the classroom, but I don't hear any of them agreeing with her, they all just leave the class trying to ignore her. I don't give her the time of day this time though. I just keep walking towards my next class as Nat and Luis catch up to me.

"Hey are you okay?" Nat asks, worry clouding her dark eyes as she walks beside me.

"Yeah I'm fine, Angela just makes me mad with how she acts towards people. I don't get why she would make fun of someone for having a crush." I turn to Luis, trying to smile at him despite still feeling upset. "Good news is though that you might have someone who likes you, Luis. What do you think? You think you might ask Kaley to the dance, give her a chance?" Luis looks a little uncomfortable, and he lowers his eyes so that he's not looking at me.

"No, I couldn't do that to her. I mean I would

be lying." I feel my eyes narrow in confusion at his words.

"What do you mean?" Luis clears his throat, obviously feeling super uneasy.

"Well I mean it would be leading her on. I don't really feel that way about her, and if I ask her to the dance then she will think that I do care about her that way. That would just be terrible to lie to her like that. Besides, I have someone else that I like, and-" Luis stops talking super quick, realizing he just let out a little secret.

"You have a crush on someone, Luis?" Luis' face grows bright red in embarrassment.

"W-well yeah, yeah, I've had a crush on this one girl for- for a really long time. I just never had the guts to tell her." Beside me, I can see Nat's face lighting up in her excitement. That's not surprising considering how much she enjoys love stories.

"C'mon Luis, you've got to tell us who she is." I plead with excitement, my heart pounding in my joy. Luis looks at me for only the slightest second before he lets his eyes fall back down to look at the floor.

"I-I don't really know if I can say… who it is right now- no, I don't think I can." Nat rolls her eyes in annoyance, and I gently smack her shoulder.

"Nat, knock it off. It's hard to admit something like that, even to your friends. Maybe you can describe her to us Luis, and then we can try to guess who it is?" Luis nods silently, and remains silent for an entire minute before he lifts his head back up to look me right in the eyes as he speaks.

"She is the most amazing girl in the world. She

is so sweet, and gentle, everything feels better when I am around her. She's always doing her best to make sure that everyone is happy, even if she isn't happy herself. She's so confident, I think she could do anything if she sets her mind to it." Luis' eyes sparkle as he looks at me, telling me about this girl. He must truly care about her. Why does my heart sting listening to this? Why do I feel so sad while my friend is telling me about someone he likes? "She is always trying to help me come out of my shell, she has helped me with so many things since I met her. And she is the most beautiful girl I have ever met, nobody else compares to her. If I could only paint and sketch one thing for the rest of my life, it would be her, and I would never get tired of doing that. I don't think any artist would get bored with her as a model. Every minute I spend with her is a blessing, and every second I'm away from her feels like agony. I… I just want her by my side, always." I am holding back tears listening to this, and I can tell that Nat is doing the same. I place my hand on Luis' arm, trying to show encouragement.

"Tell her that Luis, any girl would kill to have someone say that to them. I would be the happiest girl in the world if someone said that to me." Luis' eyes grow wide, and a hopeful expression goes over his face, as his dark eyes look deeply into mine.

"You really think that?" I nod, really struggling to keep the tears back. Why can't a guy say something like that to me? I just have to deal with Alex and his usual cheap flirty comments. I don't get to hear poetry like that. Luis takes a deep breath, as if trying to gain courage. "Well honestly

Colomba, the girl I was talking about is…well, she's- umm…" Luis' face glows red again, and it looks like he's about to throw up in his fear before he speaks again. "Oh here's my next class. I'll see you guys later." And without another word, he rushes into the classroom as if a monster is chasing him. I look over at Nat to see her eyes burning with anger and annoyance at what Luis just did.

"Who do you think he was talking about Nat?" Nat's annoyed expression towards Luis running away quickly switches to annoyance towards me. She stares at me for a moment, as if trying to see if I am joking or not before she rolls her eyes at me.

"I swear Birdy, how can you still be this blind?" Nat walks away from me and into her next class without any explanation for what she means. She leaves me with far too many questions still swirling around in my mind. I know that I am not the best when it comes to understanding things about love, but I'm not a mind reader, I don't know how to tell what someone is thinking or feeling. I get to my next class, still feeling confused by what just happened.

Chapter Four
Luis-
My Final Soldier

My face is buried in my hands as I sit at my desk, I am too embarrassed by what just happened to show my face to the world. I can't believe what I just did. I revealed to Colomba how I feel about her, without telling her that I was talking about her. I was so close to telling her how I really feel, and then I chickened out like I always do. Why do I have to be such a coward? I should have told her how I feel ages ago, but I am a coward, I can't hide from that fact. How else would you describe a person who can't even tell the person they love how they truly feel? I've been hiding behind my fear for around three years now, I need to change or else I'm going to always live in regret.

Well, I won't need to worry about that for long, things are about to change for me, and everybody else. I can see that my plan is already starting to move forward. I just need one more person to be my final soldier for my plan, and I believe that I have found her. I usually watch the person to see if they are made fun of a lot before I choose them, and I only saw Kaley getting teased once, but I know that I want to get this plan over with. I have no more patience left, this needs to be done now. Besides, I can hear people whispering to each other about what happened, telling each other about some "secret" she has that was in the note that Angela read. I have no idea what this secret could be, but that doesn't really matter to me, she will fit into my plans perfectly I just know it. I can't let anything distract me now, I have a soldier to speak to.

The teacher gives us an assignment for today, which I quickly finish before asking if I can go to the bathroom. Thankfully, the teacher allows me to go, and I make my way to the bathroom without any difficulty. I get there to find nobody else inside, locking the door, I place my hand on the Crow Medal and Shadow appears, perched on top of one of the bathroom stalls. Her black eyes glare down at me with disappointment and misery.

"So, you are actually doing this? You are actually going to try and defeat Silver Dove and force her to reveal her identity to you." She slowly shakes her feathery head at me. "I cannot believe this. In all my years as the guardian of these magical pins, I have never had something like this happen. Silver Dove and the Crow have always worked together, they have never gone against each other like this. How can you do this to her? Where have I failed you to let you think that this is the way to solve your problems?" I glare right back at her, letting her see the misery I feel.

"You didn't fail me, the world did. The world

has failed me almost every single day of my life. I know that the world won't help me, so I'm helping myself. I've been in pain and struggled all my life, but nobody helped me. If they won't help me now, then I will use whatever power I have to make sure I don't get hurt again. If doing this will get me where I need to go, then I'll do it and I won't regret a second of it. It's time for me to finally win something in my life, instead of constantly being the loser. Now transform me Shadow, there's a lot that needs to get done today." Shadow fluffs out her feathers in annoyance at my words.

"You make yourself the loser with the decisions you make. It doesn't seem like that is going to change." My eyes grow wide in shock at her words, and I'm not given a chance to respond before she starts flying around me faster and faster until she is nothing but a black blur. I blink my eyes, and when I open them, I see myself in the mirror as the Crow. My heart aches a little when I think about what Shadow just said. She has always been so kind to me, always looking out for me. Shadow has always been like the mother I had lost all those years ago. I want to listen to her, I hate disappointing her, but that won't get me to where I need to be. I want her to be proud of me, but I can't let myself be distracted by her words. I have a mission to complete.

"Shadow, find Kaley." I whisper this in the empty room, and I feel it as Shadow separates herself from me. Through my closed eyes I can see things in her perspective. She flies through the hallway as a shadow on the ground. She keeps going until she makes it to one specific classroom. Flying underneath the door, she finds Kaley among the other students. She is trying to hide the view of her face to the other students so that none of them will see how upset she is since she can hear people talking about her right now.

Shadow flies into her hurting heart, and I'm ready for my plan to begin.

Hello Kaley.

Kaley jumps a little in her seat, and she can hear some people laughing at her for this, but she doesn't care. She's too busy being terrified by the voice in her head.

What's going on? You're the Crow aren't you? I've heard people say you speak in people's heads, but why are you talking to me?

I'm definitely lucky to have someone like her for this final part of my plan. She's quick to figure out what's going on and gets straight to the point. I think we are going to work really well together.

Yes, I am the Crow, and I have a little proposition for you.

I can feel her heart racing as she waits impatiently for me to explain. Yes, I definitely chose the right person for this.

People have hurt you today, and people have been getting in my way for a few years now. Perhaps we can work together to make them stop. I can make them stop hurting you, and you can help me get what I need as well. How does that sound?

Kaley thinks to herself about how she would normally turn me down in a second, but today has been different. Today, people have hurt her, and from my experience with tempting people with these powers, people are more likely to do something terrible when they have been hurt. People are more likely to make terrible or stupid decisions when they are hurting, just like I can tell Kaley is about to do right now.

The bell ending the class rings, and Kaley tries to act naturally as she grabs her stuff and walks out into the hallway with everyone else. She can still hear people whispering about her as she begins to walk down the halls. Kaley also hears someone shout out something very mean to her. When she hears that, her mind is made up.

Please give me whatever powers you can. I want to make them suffer for hurting me.

I chuckle to myself as I hear this. She is being just as simple to trick as all the others.

Alright, go to somewhere private so I can transform you. We don't want everyone to figure out what's going on too quickly, we need to be careful with it this time. Trust me though, you will still get your revenge. You will make everyone pay for speaking so badly about you.

Kaley smiles at this, feeling as if she finally has a friend in this bad situation, as she gets out of the crowd heading to their next class and opens the door to a janitor's closet. Even though nobody really notices her doing this, she can still hear people talking about her and spreading more rumors about the note she passed this morning. As she hears this, it just makes her more sure about the decision she is making. Now, in her mind, she knows that she is doing the right thing for herself. She can't let people keep talking about her like that, she needs to defend herself. And if defending herself involves getting powers from me and causing some chaos, then she is ready and willing to do it. She silently wonders what powers I will give her, hoping that it will be something cool. I do have something in mind for her, something that will really help me with my mission today. It probably isn't as cool as she is hoping for, but it is something that will be useful. It might also make some people get a taste of their own medicine, which she will probably enjoy so she shouldn't complain. If she does try to complain, I can just threaten to take her powers away, that would get her back in line, I'm sure of it.

She closes the door, and I begin her transformation. If anybody in the hallway had been paying attention, they would have noticed a bright light coming from underneath the door, but nobody does. They are all too busy worrying about their own pathetic lives. That's about to change though, they are about to pay attention, because some changes are coming their way.

Chapter Five
Colomba-
Something is Wrong

The hallways are just as packed as always, but I somehow manage to get to my locker without any issues so that I can get some of my books out for my next class. A constant hum of voices surrounds me as everyone chats with their friends as they walk to class. I am silent and alone though since Nat and Luis have classes on the other side of the school now, but that's okay, I'm fine with being alone for a little while. Someone else apparently doesn't think the same though, since my alone time is interrupted when someone leans against the locker next to me, giving me a flirty grin that has become an almost constant annoyance to me in this school. It takes all my self-control to not roll my eyes when I see Alex looking down at me, a hopeful look in his eyes. Why couldn't I have the power to turn invisible? That would really come in handy at times like this. Please let me just disappear right now.

"Hey Colomba, how are you doing?" I release a soft sigh, trying to calm myself before speaking to him. I should be ruder to him, but I can't find it in myself to be mean to him or anyone. Practically everyone in the world is exhausting me with all the stuff I deal with as Silver Dove, sometimes I wish I could be mean to them, but I know that it wouldn't be right for me to do that.

"Hi Alex." I grab the books I need and close my locker.

"What are you up to?" Alex asks, and I can't help but look at him like he's an idiot.

"Umm… I'm heading to class, just like everyone else." I start walking to class again, but sadly Alex starts walking along side me.

"That's no problem, I can walk and talk at the same time." I hold back saying that I wish he couldn't walk or talk. I stay silent, so Alex apparently decides that he should continue the conversation.

"I wanted to apologize for what happened earlier today with the roses, I just- you know, forgot." I glare up at him, feeling so annoyed that I don't even bother to sound calm and polite.

"You forgot that I am very allergic to roses, and it makes me feel sick and awful? For a guy constantly trying to go out with me, you don't seem to know anything about me, or try to remember anything that you have learned about me. That's not a very good sign there. I think most people would think it's a huge red flag." Alex is so stunned by my words, that he stops walking for a second before easily catching up with me.

"C'mon Colomba, that was just an accident, you know that I would never try to hurt you or make you uncomfortable." This time, I do roll my eyes.

"Well for a guy who isn't trying, you are succeeding a lot." He looks hurt by my words, but he is still dumb enough to keep talking.

"That's not fair Colomba, you can't blame me for an accident. I didn't mean to do it." I groan softly.

"Whatever Alex." I'm about to step into my next class when Alex steps in front of me, an unfamiliar look on his face. He almost looks like he is about to beg to me to keep talking to him. That's really strange to see from a guy as proud as him. I stop to hear him out, but I'm only doing it because he's blocking the door. If I had any other option, I would walk past him right now and get to class.

"Colomba please, please just listen to me for a second." His eyes are pleading with me, as if he would do anything to finish this conversation with me. It's a bit creepy seeing a guy like Alex acting this way. I sigh softly, knowing that I'm going to have to listen to him begging when all I want is to get away from him.

"Alright fine, just say what you want so I can go to class. I have a lot of stuff I need to do today." He smiles softly, almost as if he is grateful that I'm giving him this opportunity. What is going on with this guy today? This is just plain weird.

"Colomba, you know I've liked you the moment I saw you back in freshman year, but every time I've asked you out you've always said no." His voice is calm and gentle, a far cry from how he usually speaks to me or anyone else. He actually sounds like a reasonable human being; unlike the arrogant jerk he usually sounds like. "I want you to just give me one chance so that I can show you how great I can be towards you. I want us to date. What do you say? Want to go to the dance with me tonight?"

Wow, I'm actually stunned by his words. He actually seems genuine with all this. I almost want to forgive him, but then I remember all the things he has done before. I think about how he has hurt Luis countless times, how he has been so pushy with me over the three years we have known each other, how he won't respect it when I tell him no, and that even though he says he cares about me he can't even remember something so simple like I am allergic to roses. This guy is toxic, and I can't let someone like him in my life. My happiness would be over if I let that happen. He does not deserve a chance with me, and I don't have to give him a chance. No matter how much he may want it, I don't have to give it to him. I make my own choices, and my choice is to not let someone as mean, pathetic, and annoying as him in my life. I need to value my happiness in life over being kind with someone who doesn't deserve my kindness.

I look up into his hopeful eyes, and I watch that hope fade away as I shake my head at him.

"No Alex. I'm not going to go out with you, I will never go out with you. I don't want you talking to me or being around me, let alone date you. You have been cruel to my friends, and you don't respect anything I say or feel. When I do date someone, it will be with someone who actually cares about me-"

"But I do care about you!" Alex interrupts, his eyes pleading with me again. "I can prove it, I-"

"No, no you don't Alex." My voice is soft, but it is stern, almost like I am scolding a kid for doing something stupid. "If you truly cared about me, you would pay attention to what I have to say, you would respect me when I tell you know, you would remember things about me, and you wouldn't hurt my friends. Why would I want to be with a guy who beats up one of my best friends? You have hurt Luis more times than I could ever guess. He is such a great guy, and you treat him like a bug under your foot. I would have to be nuts to want to go out with a guy as terrible as you. Now just let me get to class." His shock quickly disappears as anger enters his gaze. Alex glares down at me as if he is looking at someone who has betrayed him, like he is looking at an enemy. I want to back away from him, but I can't let him see my fear, that would mean he wins. Even though I know this, I am terrified that he is going to try and hit me.

"So you are saying no to me because of that freak?" He voice is a menacing growl, and it takes all my willpower to not run away like a coward. "You're really choosing him over me?" I can feel my hands shaking a little in fear, seeing the fury he has in his gaze.

From the corner of my eye, I notice someone in a dark hoodie walk up behind Alex, but I don't let my gaze leave Alex. I'm almost afraid that if I turn away from him now, he might hit me. I don't let my fear control my words though, I make sure that what I say will hurt, because I am telling him nothing but the truth. If he hears the truth in the most painful way as possible he might finally give up on me.

"Yes Alex. I would rather be friends with Luis than ever go out with you. He means more to me than you. Luis is better than you in every way. He is so sweet, and fun, and he actually cares about me, unlike you. So just let me pass because I am not going to change my mind, ever." Alex's hands clench into fists at his side, and I can't help but flinch when he quickly lifts his hand up. He does not strike me though, he only points at my face.

"Do you like him?" I fall silent at his words, feeling a little confused with myself. I honestly don't know the answer to that question. Luis has always been there for me since the day I met him, even when times were tough for the both of us. He is so sweet to me and is always trying to help me or cheer me up. He is so creative, fun, and smart. He's always working on interesting projects, and he talks about them with such passion that you just get dragged in and feel so happy for him. Any girl would be lucky to have a guy like him in their lives. I don't know if he wants me though. I mean, he's never told me if he feels that way about me, he has only acted as a friend towards me, a really good friend though. I might not be the one for him. I mean, we have known each other for ages now, if he truly cared about me that way he would have said something by now.

I can't reveal that to Alex though, or he might hurt Luis again. I'm sure he has hurt Luis before just because we are friends, so he would do something truly terrible if I said that I like him. I am so happy that Luis kept being my friend even though he always had the risk of being hurt by Alex. I am so lucky to have someone like him in my life. Behind him, the person in the black hoodie is getting closer. What on earth are they doing? Can't they see that Alex is being aggressive, why would they want to get closer to him when he is acting like this?

"I like him better than I would ever like you." Alex's face grows red with rage as the person in the black hoodie gets right behind Alex. He opens his mouth as if he is about to yell at me, but a strange look comes across his face, almost as if he is afraid of something. Like something absolutely terrifying is happening, yet there isn't anything strange around us. A pained look comes over his face, as if he's trying to hold back something, but whatever is trying to get him is winning. What is going on? Maybe I can just sneak around him so I can get to class. Just as I gather my courage to try and do this, Alex apparently loses to what was trying to get him since he screams out for the entire world to hear.

"I still sleep with my teddy bear from when I was a baby!" All eyes turn to us, looking at Alex with confusion. What did he just say? Everyone is silent as we all wonder if we actually heard him say that. And I have to say that I feel the same way; what is going on? Alex looks absolutely horrified that he said that out loud. Why on earth would he say something like that out loud? As I wonder this, I notice something on his hand, a large black thing is wrapped around his wrist. It looks unnatural and slimy. Almost like a black tentacle made out of black sludge. I follow the tentacle to see that it is attached to the person with a black hoodie, but I can't see their face underneath. The tentacle is coming out of the sleeve where their hand should be. My stomach turns at the sight of it, and I want to throw up, but I thankfully hold it back.

Oh no. No, no, no, no. This can't be happening. The Crow didn't make another one of his little creations, did he? He told me that he was stopping with his plan. He lied to me! I know that I shouldn't be surprised, but I am so disappointed in him. How could he do this? He said that he loves me, so how could he lie to my face like this? He promised me that things will be okay, but he lied! I almost feel like my heart is breaking, knowing that he lied to me even though he said that he loves me. How could he lie to someone he loves? What kind of monster is he to do this? The answer to that question immediately pops into my head. He's the kind of monster to give people powers so that they can hurt people. He's the kind of monster that enjoys causing people pain. I don't have time to pity myself any more since the tentacle around Alex's wrist seems to tighten on him and a pained look comes over his face before he shouts out again.

"I still wet the bed every once in a while after I've had a nightmare!" This time, the entire room breaks out in laughter. The entire class is pointing and laughing at him. Absolute fury is in Alex's eyes, but he doesn't say anything, he doesn't even move. I can see his body shaking, as if he is trying to move but he is being forced to hold still.

I look around Alex so that I can face the

strange person that seems to be controlling Alex.

"Stop this! What are you doing to him?!" The strange creature only laughs along with everyone else as I see the tentacle tighten its grip on his wrist again. The same strange look comes over Alex's face, almost like he is trying to hold something back, but he doesn't succeed. As I watch him break, he screams into the hallway, making all the people laughing at him suddenly grow quiet as they open their eyes wide in shock.

"I hate my life!"

Chapter Six
Luis-
Truths Revealed

"I hate my life!" Everyone falls still at that remark, too shocked to move. Everyone looks at each other, as if questioning whether or not they heard that right. Hidden in the boy's bathroom, I can see my mouth hanging open in shock reflected in the mirror.

What just happened? Did he really say that? Alex hates his life? Out of everyone I know in this school, how could he hate his life? He's the one constantly making everyone else miserable; plus he's the one who is popular, rich, and all the girls think he's good looking. Why would he be the one to hate his life, when he makes everyone else hate theirs?

"I hate everything about it!" With my soldier's tentacle still around his wrist, he continues to shout out his secrets. "Things are fine at school, but when I get home everything is terrible! Everyone is afraid of me at school, I make sure of that, so nobody messes with me. At home though, my dad never leaves me alone!" I see tears starting to flow down Alex's cheeks, and through my soldier's mind, I can feel his body relaxing in her grip, almost as if finally revealing this secret is helping him feel better about what he is saying. "My dad is the worst! I always have to be the best! Even though I do so much, nothing I do is ever good enough for him!" Alex's pained eyes suddenly grow softer as he looks at Colomba who is staring at him with both horror and pity. "But what makes it worse is that I'm never good enough for someone I care about." His voice is now softer, as if the anger is leaving him as he looks at Colomba. "Since I have kept up the act to make people afraid of me, she sees me as a monster, and I probably am one. I want her so badly, but I get rejected because she would rather hang out with one of the people I make fun of all the time than me! One of the people I see as nothing! How could a nothing person like him be better than me?!" The anger has returned, and that anger is directed at Colomba. I am glad though that she is showing anger to at what Alex just said about me.

Alright, this was fun at first, but I won't let him get angry at Colomba because of me. I don't want to see what would happen to her if he gets any angrier. I speak into my soldier's mind.

Time to move on to the next target, my soldier. There are so many more secrets that need to be revealed. You have done enough with him.

I can feel a smirk form on the lips of my soldier

underneath their hood, knowing that I'm telling the truth and that there are so many more people that need to feel the power she now possesses.

Yes Sir.

She lets her tentacle fall off of Alex's wrist, and the other students finally seem to notice it and start screaming at the sight of it. Everyone is screaming, except for Colomba, she just glares at my soldier as they walk out the door as if nobody has noticed anything wrong even though the class is screaming behind her. Colomba glares at them, obviously knowing that they are one of my creations. She knows that I lied to her. The last time I was around her as the Crow, I said that I would stop doing all this. I had made it sound like I would stop giving people powers and would join Silver Dove's side, I know what it sounded like. I didn't mean it like that though. I meant that I would stop with my original plan and go after Silver Dove instead. I couldn't tell anyone at the time what my plan was, not even her. It hurt having to lie like that to her, but it needed to be done. She'll understand… someday… I hope. Looking at the anger and betrayal in her eyes right now though, I wouldn't be surprised if it took a long time to get her to forgive me, maybe she never will.

It will be worth it though, she will see. With Silver Dove on my side, I can make things better for everyone, even her life will get better. Once she sees that, then she will forgive me and all will be right with the world. Then things will be perfect, then I can finally truly be happy. I'm sure she can be happy in that new world too, hopefully she can be happy with me.

My soldier goes down the hall, walking calmly even though the entire classroom is screaming in terror behind her. I can't help but smile right now; she is doing very well so far. I picked the right person to help me complete my mission with Silver Dove. Kaley will do what is necessary, she has enough anger in her to do anything I tell her to.

The people in the class are already telling the world about you, my little soldier. Let us show them the danger they face if they are stupid enough to speak about you.

My soldier's lips are pulled up into a rather disturbing smile, one that sends shivers down my spine even though I know I am the one controlling her. She is ready to make them all suffer for how they hurt her. She feels that if they want to spread her secrets around, then she will do what she can to make them reveal their secrets to the world.

Yes Sir. It's time to make them pay for what they have said and done to the both of us.

Without another word, she suddenly disappears from the hall, like a ghost, leaving no trace of herself behind. She knows who her next target will be, now she just needs to find them and make them pay for their sins. She is ready to cause chaos.

Chapter Seven
Colomba-
Finding My
Prey

Everyone in class is freaking out. The creature the Crow has created just left the room, and all around me people are screaming, crying, and standing still in silent, horrified shock. I know that I should follow after that thing and transform into Silver Dove so that I can fight it, but I need to make sure that everyone is alright first. Sadly, that means I have to talk with Alex since he seems to have been their first victim. Looking up at him, he is not freaking out like everyone else, he is just calmly staring down at me as if the weight of the world has just been lifted off his shoulders.

"Alex, are you okay?" Alex smiles at me, but not his usual flirty, confident grin. No, this smile is calm and even a little sad. It is almost as if he is trying to smile just to make me feel comfortable. That doesn't seem right though. Alex isn't the kind to hide his feelings to make someone feel better, he's the type who would only show the side of himself that he wants you to see. This feels so strange, but also nice to see. It feels like he actually cares in this moment.

"Yeah, yeah, I think I'm alright. At least I will be soon." I nod at that, it makes sense. I wouldn't feel alright only a minute after revealing some of my biggest secrets to the world. That at least seems to be what that creature's power is, making people reveal their secrets if they are touching you. That is a pretty scary power to have, not going to lie. I'm a little shook, imagining what kind of mess they can create by making everyone spill their secrets out to the world.

"It's okay, you just sit down and try to relax." I lead Alex over to an empty desk while the rest of the class runs out of the room in terror, all running off to either leave the school or hide. "I'm sure that whoever that was won't go after you now since they've already gotten you already. You're safe."

The room is now empty besides the two of us, and I don't really feel comfortable being alone with Alex. I know that he won't do anything right after all that, but I still don't want to be around him right now. I have too many bad memories with him to ever want to be alone with him. No matter he says, sometimes you can't change how you feel. If you hurt someone for long enough, trust just can't be built again.

"I've got to get going Alex, I need to hide in case they come back and try to go after me. Just keep yourself safe." I start heading to the door when a soft, pleading voice speaks from behind me.

"Colomba?" I look back at Alex, seeing a truly pitiful creature looking up at me with eyes that look like they are begging me to stay with him. "All the things I said when that thing touched me, I meant it, all of it. Everything about you… it was all the truth." I lower my gaze from his. I know what he wants, he wants me to say that it's alright and that I feel the same way about him, that I'll give him a chance, but that isn't going to happen. Not after everything he has done. I can forgive, but I can't forget.

"Yes, I know Alex, but it doesn't make up for how you treat everyone. I don't care how you feel about me, if you act like that towards others, I would never be with you. Goodbye Alex." I turn away from him and run out the door, but that didn't let me hide from the look of misery I saw on his face as I left. The look of someone who just had their heart absolutely shattered with only a few words. My soul aches knowing that I caused that pain, but I can't let someone like him into my life, knowing that he will just go back to who he was before and hurt my friends. No matter how painful it is for him, I don't always have to be kind, I don't always have to be merciful with my words, I don't always have to keep giving chances to people who don't deserve it, and I don't always need to be the good guy all the time. I can be honest with myself and others even if it hurts. It's okay to hurt every once in a while if it means I get to grow.

Running through the halls, I can tell that most people don't know about this new danger we all face since it is way too quiet. Usually everyone is screaming and running around when one of the Crow's newest creations is running around. I need to get things straightened out before the entire school starts panicking. It doesn't take long for me to find an empty bathroom to transform into. When I am done, I usually burst out of the room all super dramatic after I transform, but for now I need to be a bit sneaky, so I just walk out of the room and try to not let the door hit my wings on the way out. It's honestly really hard to do when you have giant wings sticking out of your back, it's super inconvenient. Why can't they just make bigger doors? It would make life so much easier for those of us with super big wings coming out of our backs. Then again, the Crow and I are the only ones in the world with giant wings coming out of our backs, so I guess nobody really cares about changing the door sizes just for us. I get it, but it still makes me a little sad. I would like some consideration for my problems in this school considering I'm saving everyone's butts all the time. Oh well, that's a fight for another day, today I need to focus on this fight.

I kick those thoughts out of my mind so that I can focus on what is important now; finding whoever this is that the Crow has transformed. I wander through the halls, trying to be as quiet as possible so that I can hear any sign of something bad. The person he transformed did go this way, and they were walking super slow, so they can't have gotten far. So where on earth can they be?

"Silver Dove!! Silver Dove!!" I feel my feathers fluff out in surprise on my wings, a not very comfy feeling I'll tell you what. Turning around, I am greeted to the sight of several people running down the hallway with fear in their eyes. The instant I see that terror, I can tell that they know where my target is.

"You've seen them, haven't you? Where are they?" Thankfully, I am not dealing with a bunch of complete idiots, so they know what I'm talking about. The one who makes it to me first, points back down the hall.

"They're in the art room! You've got to go there now! They're doing some weird, crazy stuff to Nicki!" I don't waste another second. Taking off, I soar down the hallway, sending papers and such flying around me. It only takes me seconds to reach the art room, and when I look inside, I am met with a very creepy scene.

The person with the black hoodie is standing in the middle of the room, all the art desks are scattered across the room, like everyone had quickly pushed them to the center of the room in their hurry to get away. From the sleeves of the black hoodie the black, sludgy tentacles have weaved their way around the room, like they are trying to touch every bit of it to search for a new target. One tentacle though does have its target in its grasp. Some girl I don't know, who is apparently named Nicki according to that person a second ago, has the tentacle wrapped around her upper arm. She has the same pained expression on her face Alex had as she is screaming out her secrets to the world.

"I take my little brother's candy all the time and blame it on my other brother to get him in trouble when I get bored!" The girl shouts as tears of embarrassment go down her face. The person in the black hoodie just chuckles at this, enjoying their misery, before they ask a question in a menacing voice.

"Where is Angela?" The girl gets that pained look on her face again, but this person's power must not be to only have people tell their secrets, but to also tell the truth, because after only a second of struggle the girl yells out.

"She's in Ms. McGraph's English class." The person with the black hoodie laughs as I try to slowly sneak up on them, being careful not to touch any of the tentacles scattered all throughout the room.

I raise my sword, trying to get ready to make my move. I move silently through the room, so that she won't notice me, but the girl she is holding onto betrays me by letting her eyes looks behind the creature in the black hoodie. The creature looks back at me, and I can finally see their face clearly, and I regret seeing it.

There really isn't even a face there under that hood. All there is under the hood is just this blob of the same slimy black sludge that the tentacles are made of. The slime seems to be constantly moving on the face. This thing doesn't have a nose, mouth, eyes, or any other thing you usually expect to see on a face. All there is, is the black mess. Even though there aren't any eyes on that face, I can tell somehow that this thing is glaring at me. I feel my stomach churn just looking at this thing.

"Oh, that's just all kinds of nasty." I whisper to myself as I stare at the disgusting thing I'm looking at. From somewhere on that thing's face, it releases a cold chuckle before I blink, and it is gone. I look around but I can't see any hint of that creature, not even a single tentacle is in sight. The person it had been holding is shaking in fear as they also look around the room, wondering if their tormentor is still somewhere in the room.

Okay, so apparently this creature either has the power to turn invisible or teleport somewhere. I wave my sword around me, seeing if I hit one of its tentacles or something, but it seems that nobody is around me. Alright, it's not here and I just look a bit silly waving my sword around like an idiot. Wait, the creature was asking where Angela is, I just need to go where Angela is and I'll be sure to find this thing.

Rushing out of the room, I open my wings and fly down the hall, knowing that Ms. McGraph's room is on the other side of the school. As I soar through the halls, I try and think about why this creature specifically asked for Angela. I'm guessing it has something to do with the fact that the people the Crow transforms usually go after the people who were making fun of them. It's not hard to believe that Angela would make fun of someone, so I'm guessing that's what's going on here. My heart stops for a moment when I realize the obvious; it must be Kaley.

It makes sense that it would be her. I mean, the person in the hoodie is targeting Angela and Angela was the person who spread around Kaley's secret, whatever that secret could be. Everyone is apparently talking about it, but I haven't heard anything, nor do I want to. She can keep her secrets if she wants to, I don't want to share in spreading someone's misery. And also, this person's superpower seems to be having the ability to force people to reveal their secrets. The Crow has always given his people ironic superpowers, usually having something to do with why they were getting bullied. With how everyone seems to be gossiping about Kaley lately, it would make sense that the Crow would give her that power. I just need to find her and talk to her, just like with everyone else. She isn't like the Crow, I can talk to her and she would probably tell me the truth. I'm still pretty mad that he lied to my face about stopping all of this. He said he loves me, why would he lie to someone he says he loves?

I almost fall on the ground since my wings stop flapping in terror as I realize something. This person can make someone reveal their biggest secrets, and what is my biggest secret? This person could make me reveal who I really am to the entire world. Oh my gosh, this could be bad, like really, really bad. If I am lucky it will only be me and her in the room when I blab my secret out, but that would also mean that the Crow would be listening in since he watches through the eyes of the people he transforms. So, both of them would know my secret. I would have to be the luckiest person alive to not be touched by her when I try to convince her to get rid of the powers he gave her.

Even though I know it's not the best idea to think about it, I wonder what is likely to happen if the Crow does find out who I am. Would he try to wreck everything in my life as revenge for me defeating him all those times with all the other people he has transformed? I would be angry with me if I was in his shoes, but I can only imagine how he would act towards me if he knows my secret. He could try to hurt everyone I care about; my dad, Nonna, Nat, and Luis, they could all be hurt because of me.

A little bit of hope rises in my chest as I think of something that might make things better for me. The Crow said that he loves me. He may have lied to me about this, but he has done other things to show how much he cares about me. The Crow has tried to protect me whenever he saw me in danger, maybe if he finds out who I really am he might have a change of heart and things can be different. Maybe he will join my side if he knows who I really am. Maybe I can help him get rid of all this hate he feels, and teach him how to use his powers to actually help people. My heart turns to ice when I realize what could also happen. As soon as he sees who I am, his love can turn into hate, and he does whatever he can to ruin my life. I sigh as I let these thoughts leave my mind, I need to focus on the battle I am about to fight. I can't let my fear distract me.

Whatever may happen to me, I can't let her run wild in this school. No matter what happens to me, I need to keep everyone safe. That is what I have to do. This is what I am meant to do as Silver Dove. That is my job. Honestly, I wish things could be different, but this is how it has to be. This is my responsibility.

I turn a corner, knowing that I am close to my target. It's time to get started.

Chapter Eight
Luis-
Kaley's Revenge

My soldier quietly opens the door to Ms. McGraph's classroom, where she was told Angela would be. The girl who told her this is one of Angela's little followers who tries to copy every single thing she does, so she probably was telling the truth when she said Angela would be here. If she follows everything Angela does, it would make sense that she would know her class schedule.

Even though class has already started, nobody really pays attention to the strange person who just walked in, they just continue either taking notes about what the teacher is saying or playing on their phones. My soldier scans the room, until they can see the bleached blonde head of her target. Angela is sitting in the back row, playing on her phone and not even trying to hide it like the others. My soldier slowly and quietly makes their way around the room until they get to the back, walking right behind Angela. Through my soldier's eyes, I can see that Angela is on A-Streamer now, the social media site everyone in the area seems to use. She looks at what Angela is typing, and I can see that she's spreading more gossip about other people. I can feel my soldier's body tense up with anger at seeing that, while Angela chuckles softly to herself, not knowing what is right behind her. I let myself say some encouragement to my little soldier.

Maybe it's time for her to tell everyone some gossip about herself. She's always talking about others, but maybe people need to find out more about her. What do you think?

My little soldier only smiles at that question as she lets one of her tentacles wrap around Angela's throat. I can hear Angela gasp in shock at feeling this strange, slimy thing on her throat. That surprise quickly changes to fear as the tentacle is completely wrapped around her throat. I feel Angela shudder as she tries to fight the urge that my soldier's touch is making her want to do. It doesn't take long for her to lose that fight though.

Angela stands up and yells out for the entire class to hear her.

"I hate myself!" The room grows silent as they all look at Angela in surprise for a moment before a few people start giggling. Even the teacher looks like they are holding back a chuckle at the moment. Angela tries to keep her mouth closed, but she can't resist my creature. It's so beautiful seeing this horrible person struggling and feeling the pain she has given so many other people. It's beautiful to finally see some karma. Everyone keeps staring at her in silence as she breaks down and continues spilling out her secrets. "I never feel pretty enough, so I'm constantly doing stuff to change my appearance like dying my hair and buying new, expensive cloths! Nothing works though! I still don't feel pretty enough!" A single tear falls down Angela's face, and I can't tell if it's a tear of embarrassment or anger. I don't care either way though, as long as she gets to feel the misery she gives others. She is quivering in her fear at seeing all these people stare at her, now knowing her biggest secrets.

The entire class is now watching her with joy on her face, entertained by what she's doing. A few are even laughing out loud as Angela continues to speak.

"I make fun of people, mostly girls that I think are prettier than me, because I want them to feel just as bad about themselves as I feel about myself! I just want the world to feel just as bad as I do!" More tears are now streaming down her face like a small waterfall. Nobody cares about her tears though, they are just so happy seeing her so miserable. Even though most of the people in the class are distracted by what Angela is saying, one person notices my creature behind Angela. When they see the tentacle wrapped around Angela's throat, they let out an ear-piercing scream to makes all the joy everyone was feeling disappear in a second. Everyone lets their eyes leave Angela to look at the screaming girl, wondering what on earth is going on with her, but when she points at the tentacle, the entire room breaks out into chaos. Everyone knows what this strange sight means, it means that I'm back and I'm ready to cause problems. I'm glad they all recognize my signs, and know that they should be afraid of them.

People immediately start running out the door, but my creature's tentacles grab a few more people as they go. As soon as she has a grip on them, they stop running and start spewing out their darkest secrets. My creature holds on to Angela though, not willing to let her go yet. Angela is the cause of her misery, and she wants to make her suffer the most. The class has now left besides the few that she has at her mercy. She steps in front of Angela, wanting to look her in the face as Angela reveals all her dark secrets to my little soldier.

"I buy expensive clothes and purses just to make other people feel poor! I don't even like how they look most of the time! I just want to make everyone feel bad! I think they deserve to feel bad because they are happier than me!" Angela looks into my creature's eyes with the most pitiful gaze I have ever seen. Her eyes are full of tears as she stares at my creature with the face of someone who has lost all hope, someone who is begging for mercy.

In my soldier's mind, I can tell that they are almost tempted to let them go when they see that pitiful look in Angela's eyes, but then they remember who they are dealing with. This is the girl who has tried ruining countless people's lives, the one who tries to make everyone miserable to build herself up, the one who caused all the problems Kaley felt that made her accept her powers from me. A girl like Angela doesn't deserve mercy, the only thing she deserves is to learn how to suffer like all the others she has made miserable. She deserves the humiliation that she feels now. She deserves every bit of horror and depression she feels right now.

As my creature enjoys the sight of this horrible human being facing karma, a sound disturbs the beauty of this moment. My creature turns around to see that the sound was the door opening, and standing in that doorway is Silver Dove, her sword held out in front of her, pointing it right at my soldier. Through the eye holes of the mask, I can faintly see Silver Dove's eyes glaring at her with absolute fury.

"Put them down Kaley." My creature's heart skips a beat, knowing that Silver Dove has figured out her identity so quickly. How did she realize it so fast? Oh well, it doesn't matter, we just need to keep moving forward with the plan. The shock doesn't last long before a smile plays across her slimy face.

"Alright, see you soon Silver Dove." And without another word, my creature does put down the people she had in her tentacles. Once that is done, she does what she was ordered to do after I gave her these powers. She disappears.

My soldier has a lot more to do before she can get caught by Silver Dove. I know it will happen sometime sooner or later, but I want Silver Dove to be worn down by that point. I need this battle to last a long time. I did not tell my soldier this, she does not know what my real plans are. She just thinks that this will be just like every other time someone has been transformed. All I told her to do was to disappear whenever Silver Dove appears, until I tell her to face Silver Dove. Only then will I finally get what I want.

Chapter Nine
Colomba-
Finding Kaley

My wings ache as I soar through the hallways, dodging crowds of people as I make my way through the school. I feel like I have been flying all day, searching for Kaley. Each time I catch up to her, she disappears again and then I have to go around searching for her again, trying to listen and hear any screaming or any other indication of where she could be. I've "found" her about ten times now, and even though I try sneaking up on her, she always realizes I'm there and disappears again.

Everyone is in a panic right now, begging for me to end this whenever I fly past, but I don't know how. I have already been at this for two hours, and I feel like I am going to pass out any second. What am I going to do if I can't find her? Can she just cause chaos forever, or will her powers fade after a while? I have no idea what will happen because of this.

My eyes grow wide underneath my mask, and I let myself land, my shoes skidding on the tile floor when I realize the obvious. She is probably disappearing and reappearing near different targets, if I can get everyone in one room then she will have no choice but to go there so that she can get her revenge on everyone.

Turning around and taking off, I fly towards the front of the school, knowing that I am about to ask the other students in this school to do something that will take a lot of bravery to do. I may be nuts to try this, but I need to do something. I have made plenty of sacrifices to save them, now they need to be brave for just a few minutes for me. After everything I have done for them, I think they can do this simple thing for me. It doesn't take long to make it to the front office. As I step into the office, I find the principal, vice principal, and the front office lady hiding behind their desks. I almost want to laugh at the fact that these people who are supposed to be leading this school are hiding like cowards while I, a student, am the one fighting the danger.

Stepping behind the principal's desk, I easily find the intercom system. Pressing the button, I can hear the static on the intercom, and I know that I can send my message out to the school.

"Everyone, this is Silver Dove. I need everyone to go to the gym. The Crow has created another one of his monsters, and I need everyone to go there for safety. This person is looking for targets and if we are all spread out throughout the school, I won't be able to find them in time. Get to the gym now or else we may never get rid of this person." I end the announcement, and I can hear the people in this office running towards the gym, following my order without a second thought. I know that the rest of the school will do the same. Even though many of them mock me when things are okay, they trust me to keep them safe when times are tough.

My heart feels heavy, knowing what I am really doing. Kaley is going after people to make them tell their secrets, if I have everyone in the same room then she will follow them and be easier to find. I'm pretty much using everyone in this school as bait for Kaley. It's not like they will be physically hurt by Kaley's powers, but if she touches them then they will definitely hurt emotionally considering they will be screaming out their secrets in front of the entire school.

I make my way to the gym myself, ready to end this fight. My sword feels heavy in my hands as I push the door open to find that a lot of people have already arrived, and more are pouring through the other doors scattered around the room. I fly into the air to get a better view of everything even though my wings hurt so much that I'm afraid they will just fall off. I've been flying around too long. Looking back at my wings, I can see some of my feathers falling off, a clear sign that I am getting too tired, and my powers are starting to fade. If I don't get some rest soon then I will be revealing my identity to the entire school. I need to end this, and I need to end this now.

I wait in silence as the gym gets more crowded as the students keep filing in. Beneath me, people are trying to get me to come down to their level, they want to talk to me, saying they are big fans, but I can't let myself get distracted by them. Many of them are taking pictures of me while the rest are chatting and laughing with their friends like nothing is wrong. I can't believe them, they're acting like this is a party and they can have a good time, it's like this is a fire drill and it's just a fun way to get out of class. I guess that they expect me to save the day and they can watch like it's a football game or something. Honestly, I feel annoyed seeing them like this, they aren't taking this seriously even though I'm risking everything to help them. Why don't they realize how serious this is? Why doesn't anyone care?

My eyes scan the crowd until I notice a dark figure in the corner. They are looking around, obviously trying to figure out what to do now that all of their prey is in one room, but I am also in that room. Without saying a word, I dive towards her, my sword held at the ready, ready to end this. When everyone sees what I am doing, they break out into cheers, but I can barely hear them, I am too focused on my target. Problem is, with everyone's attention on me, my target can see me as well. When I am only a few yards away from her, she disappears again. I am able to spread out my wings quickly enough to catch myself before slamming my face into the wall, but I am stuck to searching again.

I fly back into the air, my heart pounding and my body aching as I start looking again. My sword feels like it weighs a million pounds. It only takes a second for me to spot her again, hiding behind two girls talking to each other about what's happening, but once again, as soon as I start trying to move towards her, she disappears.

My head darts from side to side, searching desperately, and she is now on the other side of the gym next to a group of people talking. I start flying over, but I am only able to make it a few feet before she disappears again. I fly in place, my mind rushing to try and figure out what to do. All around me, everyone is talking about what is taking place in front of them, and as I watch, I notice the shape of the creature constantly moving, constantly appearing and disappearing again. As I watch her, I notice something. She is always appearing close to people who are talking and not the ones who are silently watching what's going on. Everyone is talking about what is happening, everyone is talking about her. The idea hits me, and I realize the truth. When she did her first attack against Alex, she had to walk behind him, but has been disappearing and then appearing close to others the rest of the time to get closer to newer targets. She is appearing next to those who are talking about her, she attacked Alex and then got to teleport herself elsewhere because people were talking about her. Her powers involve secrets and gossiping, so that means she can teleport to wherever someone is talking about her. I know how to end this.

"Everyone stop! She can teleport herself to whoever is talking about her! So everyone just shut up!" The entire gym falls silent at my harsh words, and I let my eyes scan the crowd, looking for Kaley. It doesn't take me long to find her dark figure trying to hide herself near the door.

No, you aren't going to hide from me that easily. Diving towards her, I slam my body into hers, the two of us crashing through the door and into the entryway of the school. Behind me, I hear people screaming and running in the opposite direction. Good, let them all get to safety, I have a fight to win.

Chapter Ten
Luis-
A Good Fight

From my soldier's eyes, I watch as Silver Dove tackles her through the door and they start fighting in the entryway of the school. I smile to myself as my soldier begs me in her mind to help her, to save her from Silver Dove who is swinging her sword at her, trying to slash at her dark tentacles. I don't respond to her though, the part of my plan involving her is over now, time to focus on the next part. She can handle this fight on her own. Everything is moving so smoothly, just like I have always wanted.

Leaving the bathroom, I start walking down the halls, and the people around me begin to scream in terror and run the other way, absolutely terrified of me. It is so beautiful to see. I love seeing them be afraid of me, but they are about to be a lot more afraid when they see what I'm about to do.

I need to get to where Silver Dove is. I have a fight to win.

Chapter Eleven
Colomba-
Everything Is
Done

Using what little strength I have left, I swing my sword back and forth as this creature keeps sending more and more of her tentacles out to try and get me. At first, I had been afraid that if I cut the tentacles that it would hurt her, but apparently, she can't feel it because I'm just cutting through these and she doesn't react at all. As soon as I cut one, it oozes some black slime onto the ground, it heals itself, and then goes right back to trying to get me again.

I need to think of a plan to get through these tentacles and get her, but my brain is too foggy from exhaustion to think of anything. What am I going to do?

While we had been fighting, we had made our way out of the entryway of the school and are now fighting on the front lawn. From the corner of my eye, I can see the other students watching the fight from the windows. Most are filming what is happening. Don't they realize how serious this is? Why are they treating this like they are watching some kind of action-packed movie? Don't they know that this is real? Don't they realize that bad things could happen if I lose this fight? Why are they all just watching this? Why won't any of them help me? Why am I always alone in these fights? Why do I always have to do all the tough things on my own?

As I think about these depressing questions, it's obvious what mistake I have made. I let myself get distracted. When I had glanced over to see that there are people filming us, I didn't notice a tentacle go around me, and now it is wrapped tightly around me throat, like it wants to strangle me. Another tentacle wraps around my hand that has my sword. It twists my wrist until I am forced to let go of the sword and I hear it clatter to the ground as I feel the magic of this creature's powers pulsing through me. My eyes grow wide in terror as I feel that, desperately praying that I can fight it.

I try so hard to keep my mouth closed that I feel my teeth aching from clenching them together too hard. Even through the slime on her face, I can tell that she is smiling as she sees me struggle. I know that I can't keep it in, I'm going to reveal my secret identity to the world. It only takes a minute of misery until I am forced to open my mouth and a single tear falls down my face as I scream out what I've been holding back for three years now.

"I hate being Silver Dove!" This creature backs away from me, recoiling their tentacle from my throat as if they are afraid of burning themselves. Did I just say that? I have been having some feelings like this for a while, but now that I've said it, I realize that it's true. I've been trying to lie to myself to say that it isn't true, but apparently, I can't hide this secret from this creature's magic. Even though this creature is no longer touching me, I keep yelling out my truth. Now that I've let it out, I kind of want to tell everyone about how I truly feel. "I hate that I was chosen to be Silver Dove! It just made everything in my life harder! I never get a break! I have school, I'm constantly training, and then I have to keep my eyes open for the Crow every second of the day?! It's not fair! I'm just a kid! I have never done anything bad! Why do I deserve this?!" I take a moment to breathe, trying to hold back the tears that are struggling to come out of me. Looking over at the other students who are still filming this, I feel so much pain and almost hatred when I look at them. I have stayed as Silver Dove this long because I need to protect them, yet they are just filming this like it's fun. Can't they see that I'm not having fun with this? I face them so that they can clearly see how I feel. Already, I can see some of them lowering their phones, no longer filming. Those are the ones who have listened to what I have said and feel compassion for me. These are only a few of them though, most of the people are still filming. I can even see a few of them laughing at my misery. How could they do this to me after everything I have done for them?

"I have done everything right in my life; so why do I constantly have to struggle and deal with this pain just to save you guys?!" I point an accusatory finger at all of them, summoning my sword back into my other hand, and the laughing immediately dies down. They know that I am merciful, usually, but I am now angrier than I have ever shown them. They know how powerful I am, they know that if they keep acting up around me, then I might snap. Honestly, it's depressing seeing the fear in their eyes right now, but also it feels a little good. It feels like I am finally feeling some respect from them. I hate knowing that they feel fear right now because of me after all these years of me protecting them, but I can't stop now. Now that I have their full attention, I keep going. "You guys are the ones causing all of this! You know that the Crow is transforming kids who are getting picked on, and yet you keep messing with them! You see what's going on, but you keep doing it because you think I will keep fixing your problems! I'm getting sick and tired of doing it though! One of these days I might just let you guys deal with it on your own!" I am lying about that, I wouldn't let people suffer just to make a point, but they don't know that. I can actually see a few of them with eyes wide in terror, thinking that I will abandon them to be hurt by one of the Crow's creatures. "You all have been filming this like I've been entertaining you instead of saving you! How can you guys just stand there and watch me suffer like this?! You act like everything is fine, but I can barely take this anymore!" I have let them see how I feel, now I just need to dig the knife in even further. "Everyone always says that they would want superpowers, but it puts so much pressure on you to get everything right and to save everyone; but I can't!!!" I take in a few more deep breaths as I whisper something more to myself than to the creature in front of me or the other students. "I can't even save myself." My heart feels like it is shattering in my chest because I know it's true, I have gone through so many bad things ever since I got these powers, and I've been able to save so many people, but I always get hurt one way or another. I look back up at this problem the Crow has created for me, and my rage instantly returns in full force. The creature flinches when I look at it again, as if my simple glare frightens it.

"And now I have to deal with you! I've heard countless people complain about how all this stuff with the Crow has been going on for too long, but nobody ever offers to help me out! The police don't even help anymore since they think I will handle it! Well, if all of you think you can do a better job then come out of your hiding spots and help out! She's right here! So come and get her! Or are you too scared to try?!" I look around, as if welcoming anyone to come help me, but my tone easily tells everyone that I am joking. Anyone who is listening to me can tell that I don't believe anyone will help. I've been fighting this war for three years now, and nobody has helped me yet. I've given up hope of ever having someone fight by my side. I am alone to fight this war.

After mocking this entire school, I look towards the creature who made me realize how I have secretly felt for so long. I am smiling at her coldly while she looks at me with discomfort and a little bit of fear.

"Well, are you going to keep fighting, or are you going to finally come to your senses and stop all the stupidity and move on with your life?!" My words are harsh, and I know she feels the anger I am putting in those words from how pained she looks. She opens her mouth like she is planning to say something, but nothing comes out. The creature clears her throat awkwardly before she speaks in a voice only slightly above a whisper.

"They were hurting me Silver Dove, I had to do something." I am usually sympathetic to people in this situation with the Crow, but right now, I am too furious to care.

"And you think that makes all of this okay?!" She cowers a little bit at my words, as if she is afraid I am going to hurt her. I would normally back off a bit when I notice something like this, but I am too riled up to calm down now. "After everything that has happened with the Crow in the couple years we have gone to school together, you think it's a good idea to join his side to get revenge?! Have you ever seen any of his people win a fight?! What were people even making fun of you for?!" She hides her face from mine as if embarrassed by the rumors people have been spreading.

"They made fun of me for liking someone who-"

"SO?!" I interrupt her, and she flinches at the sound of my anger. "If you like someone, then tell them how you feel! Who cares what other people think about it?! The only person's opinion you should care about with this, is the person you have feelings for, that's it! They are the only person who matters in all this! If they care about you too then great, if not then you move on with your life and you will find someone else! It may hurt for a while, but it won't last forever! You just need to move forward!" She looks so pitiful right now, she has practically been cowering from me as I have been yelling at her. I have been much too harsh, no matter how I feel right now, I can't let myself hurt someone else. That would go against everything I have ever stood for as Silver Dove. I need to do that even though nobody really respects me for what I stand for, but I need to forget that for now. I clear my throat to try and calm myself and soften my voice to her.

"It's okay to feel nervous and afraid to reveal your feelings to someone, I mean you are basically handing your heart over to someone in the hopes that they won't crush it. If you want to be happy though with this person, you've got to take a chance and risk being with someone and that other people might make fun of you for it. If you care about the person though, then it will be worth it." She looks up at me, a quiet sadness in her eyes. "Are you ready to try again with your life, or do you want to keep fighting? I can keep fighting forever, I think I have proven that through the years with this job."

She gives me a little half smile, knowing that my little joke at the end is the truth. All she gives me is a nod and I know what will happen. I back away from her a few steps as she closes her eyes, and a bright light comes from her, and I have to use my wing to cover my eyes until the light disappears. When the room is back to normal, I lower my wing to see that Kaley is in front of me, back to her regular self.

Kaley smiles at me, as if silently begging me to forgive her, I am only able to smile warmly back at her before something powerful hits me from the side and I am thrown to the ground, unable to catch myself in my surprise. Above me, I hear Kaley scream and I look over to where she was to see her running down the hall to get to safety, above me though are the massive fangs of one of the Crow's demon dogs. In my fear, my fist swings out, hitting it squarely on its muzzle, and it disappears into nothingness. I'm able to get myself back up just in time to see an entire pack of these dogs running through the front doors to get to me, with the Crow himself following not too far behind, making more and more of those dogs as he gets closer. The people inside the school shout hateful things at the Crow, but they instantly run and hide when the Crow glances their way. They may be brave enough to say mean things behind his back, but not to his face. Over the sound of his demon dogs growling, I can hear him laugh when he sees them run.

I need to think, I need to get these things away from the school, so nobody gets hurt by these monsters. Without another thought, I take off, flying through the air until I reach the edge of the road in front of the school, about thirty yards from the front doors with the demon dogs closely nipping at my heels. I can't go any farther than this though. Beyond the road are some neighborhoods with the woods next to it. I can't let them cause destruction to people's houses and I am too tired to try and fight them in the woods. They would just keep hiding behind trees and such and then they would jump out as soon as I think I am done. I need to be out in the open, so I know what's going on.

What is going on?! Why is the Crow here?! This guy never shows up after I have defeated one of his people. I always assumed that he just goes off to mope about his loss, but not this time I guess. Now that I am away from the school, I fly up into the air so that I can see what I am dealing with. As soon as I look though, I regret my decision. What looks like an ocean of darkness is beneath me, but when I squint, I can see that it is a giant mass of the Crow's shadow dogs.

Countless students can be seen returning to the windows now that I led them farther from the school, they are all trying to catch a glimpse of what is to come. Once again, they all look like they are expecting to see some kind of show. What do they think this is? A movie? No, this is me fighting, not only for my life, but for all of their lives too. Why can't they see that? Were they not listening to what I was just saying? Why won't anyone ever help me? My body already feels worn out having to fight with his little soldier, having to dodge her so much and fly around trying to get to her. I don't know how long I can last against an entire army of these shadowy monsters.

I don't have time to think about that now though, I have some demon dogs to fight. Sailing down into the mass of darkness, I swing my sword down towards them, trying to get as many of them as possible. I can see only a few of them disappear from my sword striking them before the enemy strikes back. One of the demon dogs grabs my foot with its fang filled mouth, and uses that to drag me to the ground where all of his other buddies pile on top of me with teeth biting at me and claws trying to tear me apart. I may not be able to get hurt with my powers, but I still feel pain, and I am in agony right now.

I scream as I feel their teeth trying to dig into me, but they can't get past my invulnerable skin. It feels like I am being crushed under their weight. All around me I hear their teeth grinding against my armor and their constant barking, whining, and howling. Through it all though, I hear one other thing that seems to make all the other sounds disappear until I hear nothing else except it. The sound of the Crow laughing at me, laughing at my misery. As soon as I hear that sound, that infuriating sound, all the pain from the demon dog's teeth, all the pain, all the misery is gone. All that's left is anger, anger at this pathetic kid who is so determined to hurt me, to hurt everyone in this school just because he feels bad about his life. He feels bad about how things are for him, so he has to take it out on everyone. All the rage I felt when I started yelling out the truth earlier with his latest soldier comes back to me all of a sudden, giving me a sudden burst of energy. Yanking my arm out of the grip of several demon dogs, I grab my sword that had fallen beside me, and I begin slashing at all the demon dogs around me.

They fade away into shadows as I strike them, but more and more come to take their place. My sword swings back and forth, trying desperately to get as many as I can, but it never seems to be enough, the Crow keeps making more to make my fight go on forever. From the corner of my eye, I can see some of my feathers start falling off of my wings again.

Oh no, no, no, no. This can't be happening! This can't happen now! I know what that means. It means that I am getting too tired, and when that happens, my powers will start to fade. I need to end this fight, and I need to end it now before my powers leave me. I can't end it if I keep trying to fight all these demon dogs though, I need to attack the source of this problem. Taking off into the air, my eyes instantly see where the Crow is among his army of demon dogs, a smudge of black hidden within the ocean of darkness. I dive bomb towards him, my sword ready to strike, ready to end this.

The Crow seems to have noticed what I am planning since several demon dogs leap up to try and get at me before I can reach him, but I just slash at them with my sword and they disappear into nothingness as I get closer to my target. Why isn't the Crow running away? He is just watching me get closer to him as calm as can be. I am almost at him, almost ready to get all this over with, but as I lift my sword to make my strike, what feels like a massive wave crashes into me and I tumble to the ground, once again getting crushed by the demon dogs. Well now the obvious can be seen, he stayed still so that I would get closer so he could get a massive group of his dogs to jump at me all at once. I am so stupid.

Once again, they use their teeth to try and tear me apart while the Crow watches on with a dark, evil glimmer of joy in his eyes. When they threw me to the ground, my sword got knocked out of my hands and is hidden someone underneath the crowd of dogs. As their teeth scrape against the metal of my armor, I feel more feathers getting ripped off of my wings and my body feels like it weighs a million pounds. I can feel myself growing weaker and weaker as I am getting more worn out by this endless battle. I can't let this go on any longer or else all will be lost.

Using all of my effort, I rip my arm out of the toothy grip of at least three of his shadow dogs, and raising my hand, summoning my sword back to me. Through the crowd of these demon dogs, I see one of them carrying the sword in its jaws, trying to bring it to its master. As soon as I start summoning it towards me, I see the creature struggle to try and hold on to it, but my magic is too strong for it. The sword flies out of its mouth, and the dog leaps to try and snatch it back out of the air, but the magic is too fast for it. My sword lands squarely back into my hand and I immediately start slashing at these beasts again even though it feels like my arm is going to pop off in my exhaustion.

My heart skips a beat when I notice something terrifying. As my sword cuts into demon dog after demon dog. My armor bracelets start to glow for a moment before they disappear off my arms like they were never there. The Crow must have noticed this too since I hear his dark, sinister laugh over the sounds of his dogs barking and howling. Is this what he's been trying to do this whole time? Is that why he made Kaley go all over the school so that I would have to chase her? Then he created an army of shadow dogs just to go after me and nobody else? He is just doing this so that I would get exhausted, and my powers would fade! He wants to figure out who I really am and then… and then what? What does he plan on doing when he realizes who I really am? Will he expose me to the school? Will he try to force me to join his side? Or worse, will he try to hurt me and my family?

I can't keep fighting him or else I will be exposed. I can't stay here or else he will just keep making new shadow dogs and I will have my powers fade. I need to just leave without getting myself hurt. I know that the Crow won't do anything to any of the other students, it's me that he's after right now. I just need to get away and get away fast so that he won't be able to find me, so that I can rest. I can't waste another second.

Flying into the air, avoiding all the dogs beneath me, I throw my sword straight at the Crow. I don't even wait to see if it hits him or not (I'm sure it won't, he'll have his dogs stop it before it gets close), but it will give me enough of a distraction to fly off. Flying as fast as I can, I can feel my feathers falling off my wings as I become more and more tired, but I can't let him find me. I fly straight into the forest across the street from my school, hoping to find some cover from his view. When I feel like I have gone far enough, I let myself land in front of a tree. Leaning against it, I feel my eyes beginning to close and I know that I am about to pass out. At least I am safe though. I can't see the Crow anywhere near me, he isn't as fast as me and he shouldn't have been able to keep up. I've lost him, and now I can finally rest. With peace in my heart, my eyes close and I am lost in the darkness as I let myself fall asleep.

Chapter Twelve
Luis-
All is Revealed

I fly through the air as fast as I can, trying desperately to make sure I don't miss her, it's not too hard to follow her though with the trail of silver feathers leading me right to her. My wings tilt from side to side as I fly through the trees of the forest. I know she landed somewhere over here, and she probably doesn't have any energy left. I could tell that she was getting exhausted, so she should be back in her normal form now. I can finally do it. I can finally see who she really is! I can finally know and then I can figure out a way to convince her to join my side. After all these years, it's all about to end, and I'm going to love every single second of it. As I pass by a small clearing, I notice something brightly colored and I can tell that it's not a part of the forest, it's the color of someone's clothing. I rush over to it, knowing that it is her.

I glance through the trees until I get close to what I am looking for. I notice the body of a person laying in the grass at the foot of a pine tree. Landing carefully, I run over in my excitement, I smile broadly as I walk around the tree and finally look down at the unmasked face of my enemy. The girl who has defeated me so many times over the last few years. I look down, expecting to gloat at their unconscious body, but the words are trapped in my throat as I see the true face of Silver Dove. My eyes are huge as I stare at her, I blink rapidly several times, hoping that I am mistaken, but the sight in front of me doesn't change. I take in a few deep breaths since it feels as if all the air has left my lungs. What have I done?

"No, no not you. It can't be you." I whisper this, almost as if I am afraid to wake her up. Laying at the foot of the tree, looking like a sleeping princess, is Colomba. Her eyes are closed, and she has a peaceful smile on her face like she is enjoying a happy dream even though her enemy is standing above her. My heart shatters a little as I think about that, I really am her enemy. I have been her friend for years, and I've loved her that entire time, and yet I have caused her so much pain. How could I do this to her? How could I do this to someone as gentle and sweet as her? I think back about everything that I have made Silver Dove go through.

I have made her fight tons of people and have caused so much chaos. I have scared her so many times and made her afraid for herself and everyone around her. Thinking back to what she said earlier when my creature touched her, I become even more upset. I made her hate the powers she's been given. Practically anyone in the world would want to have powers like hers, but because of what I have made her go through, she now hates her gift. I have made her have to work so hard to train to fight whatever I came up with, all while trying to have a normal school life and dealing with all the advanced classes she's in. I have made her go through so much, and before I knew it was Colomba, I enjoyed causing that pain to her. Now that I know who she is though, I feel so guilty. How could I do this to Colomba?

I didn't know though. I couldn't have known. I always knew that she sided with Silver Dove, but I didn't think she was her. She just never seemed the type to be a superhero. I knew that Colomba had experience with fighting and swords, but I always thought she was too gentle to use any of those skills on somebody. She's the kind of person who wouldn't hurt a fly, I never expected her to be able to fight her way through all the people I've transformed and all the shadow dogs I've created.

What do I do? I don't know what I'm supposed to do… Well, first things first, I can't leave her here in the middle of the woods. I need to get her somewhere safe. Through the trees, I can see that school is letting out for the day. People are leaving the school and getting onto buses and into their cars. Colomba and I usually take the bus together, but I don't think that's an option right now. I need to get her home safely. All I can do now is hope and pray that she doesn't wake up when I do this.

Bending over her, I gently lift her into my

arms, carrying her like I am holding the most precious thing in the world. To me, that's exactly what she is. She feels so light in my arms as I start flapping my wings so that I can fly with her. I can't take my eyes off of her as we take off from the ground. I fly over the trees and start heading in the direction of her house. I take in deep breaths, trying to calm myself so that I can think clearly. She looks so serene right now, as if she is at complete peace flying through the air like this. My heart has a crushing feeling when I realize the obvious, she looks peaceful right now in her sleep even while flying, because she is used to flying. She is Silver Dove, she has had plenty of experience flying through the sky. Flying while fighting some of the monsters I have created.

Why couldn't Silver Dove have been someone I don't know? Or better yet, why couldn't she have been someone I hate, like Angela or someone else like her? Why did she have to be Colomba? Why did she have to the girl of my dreams and my best friend?

I think back to all the times I have hurt Silver Dove with all the terrible things I have done. I caused her so much pain and misery. When I had the Taker steal what she loved the most, he took away her friends and family. And just earlier today when my newest soldier touched her and made her reveal her darkest secret, she said that she hates being Silver Dove. She said that being Silver Dove caused her so much heartache, but she's wrong. Being Silver Dove didn't cause all that, I did. I caused all the pain in her life.

My heart suddenly feels as if it is having all the weight of this moment lifted off when I realize something. I may have caused her pain in the past, but I can get rid of the pain in the future. My mind suddenly flashes back to that Valentine's Day where Shadow told me something that angered me when I first heard it, but brings me joy now. Shadow told me that those who wear the pins are destined to be together. I am supposed to end up with Colomba. Colomba and I are supposed to fall in love. My heart skips a beat when I look at her now. I have thought for so many years that I could never be worthy of her, that she would never love me back considering how pathetic I am, but no, she will love me. I can finally be with the girl of my dreams. We are destined to be together.

The only problem I can think of though with that is how will I talk to her about this? I mean, she has always stood against what I have done as the Crow… but maybe things can be different now. Once she knows that I really am the Crow, maybe she will finally listen to me and then she will join my side. Once we use our powers to make all the misery in our little part of the world stop, then she can rule over it by my side to make sure that nobody ever gets hurt again.

Thinking about how Colomba is though, that will take a lot of convincing. I mean, Colomba is an extremely kind and peaceful person, she doesn't seem like the kind to want to rule over anybody. I'm sure she can learn though, she's a smart girl. She will realize that things need to change, and we have the power to change things for the better. As Silver

Dove and the Crow, we can speak and people will listen. I can only hope that Colomba will listen to me.

Below me, I can see that I am close to her house. Letting myself get closer to the ground, I make my way to the back of her house so that I can get to the window to her bedroom. Since it is a nice day out, the window is thankfully open to let in the calm spring breeze. It's a bit difficult to squeeze through the window while still holding onto Colomba and having huge wings, but I somehow manage without hitting her head or anything. I did hit my head though, but that doesn't really matter, she got in without getting hurt, that's all that matters.

Setting her down gently on the bed, I let myself get one last look at her before I have to go. I don't really want to leave her, I want to comfort her when she wakes up since I know she will be so confused when she finds herself in her room. I can't do that though, I would only scare her more. I can't let her see me like this, it would only make it worse. I have to let this happen. Her dark hair just seems to flow off her pillow while her sleeping face looks so happy, like she is in a beautiful dream. I want to stay longer, just to be with her, but I let myself out through the same window I came in from. I will see her again tomorrow at school, and I will have a lot to discuss with her. There is so much that needs to be figured out between us. I take off into the air, already trying to plan out what I need to say to her to get her to join my side. I have a lot to think about.

Chapter Thirteen
Colomba-
What Happened

Sunlight touches my face, and I can see the light through my eyelids. The gentle feeling of the warmth from the sun wakes me up, and I open my eyes to see the light coming through the curtains of my bedroom. Oh good, I'm in my own room, for a second I had a feeling that something bad was happening. I wrap myself in my blankets and I'm about to let myself fall back to sleep when a heart stopping thought makes my eyes pop back open again in horror. Sitting up, I look around the room as if expecting to find someone there. I remember what happened right before I passed out. I had let myself rest in the forest outside of the school before I passed out, so how did I get here? I mean, I couldn't have brought myself home. Hopping out of my bed, I start pacing back and forth in my room, trying to remember more so I can figure out what happened.

I had been in the forest outside of the school, which is miles away from here, so what brought me back home? Did some random person find me in the middle of the woods and then bring me back home? Looking out the window, I can tell from how high the sun is still up in the sky, that not much time has passed since I fell asleep. I would guess that only an hour or so has passed since then. For a regular human to be able to do that, it would have taken a lot more time to find me, take me out of the woods, find out where I live, drive me home, and then drop me off in bed. It's not possible for it to have been some regular human, nobody would be fast enough. My heart skips a beat when I realize the obvious. The Crow was the one who brought me home; wasn't he?

I mean the Crow was trying to chase me, he knows where I live, and he has shown that he has feelings for me so he wouldn't want to hurt me. At least I don't think he would. So maybe he was the one who brought me back. That can't be though; why would he just leave me here if he realized who I am? He was trying to destroy me earlier today, why would his little crush mean anything if he found out I'm Silver Dove considering we've been enemies for so long? He would have done something bad while I was at that weak moment, that would be the only thing to do that would make sense for an evil guy like him.

Why would he do this? It doesn't make sense. A little crush wouldn't outweigh his hatred of me as Silver Dove. I don't understand any of this. I keep pacing the floor, trying to think, but I keep thinking of the same questions and one simple fact, that none of this makes sense. I'm so scared right now that it feels like I'm going to throw up. What am I going to do? What can I do? If I don't really know what happened, then I don't know what I'm supposed to prepare for. All I can do is keep acting like everything is normal. If I act like things are normal, then whoever got me home will have to come up to me to try and talk to me about what happened. Maybe then I could get some answers. But how do I know if someone helped me get here or not?

A thought occurs to me which helps me feel just a little bit better. The only thing that I can think about that would make sense for what really happened was that maybe I flew farther than I remember and was able to make it home before the Crow found me. That must be it. That's the only thing that makes sense with all of this craziness. I sit down on my bed, burying my face in my hands as I try to convince myself that that's what happened. I need to believe that, that's the only way that I can feel safe.

Chapter Fourteen
Luis-
Harsh Words

I am pacing back and forth in my bedroom while Shadow watches me with a patient expression, perched on my desk chair like nothing crazy just happened only an hour ago. I just finished explaining to her what I plan on doing tomorrow at school to try and complete my plan with Colomba. She had listened in silence as I went on with my plan, and let the silence stay between us for a moment after I was done. She is sitting there patiently, as if she is trying to figure out a way to say what she needs to in a gentle way. Apparently, she decides to give up on being gentle with it, and instead is her usual bluntly honest self.

"This will not go well for you Luis, if you try to do what you are planning, you will just frighten her and make her afraid of not just the Crow, but of you. She has been terrified of the Crow ever since you announced to the world that you are her enemy, and she has had countless nightmares about you. You have been the cause of all the misery within her existence for years. Do you honestly think after all that she would want to join your little crusade to frighten the town?" I am about to yell at her for insulting my plan, but then I feel my eyes narrow in confusion as something she says sticks in my mind.

"How do you know what she was thinking back then, and how do you know if she's had nightmares about me or not? She's never told me about anything like that, so how would you know?" My eyes grow wide as the obvious truth hits me. I feel as if someone has punched me in the gut as I look into the eyes of this creature I have trusted for so long. "You've known it was her the entire time, didn't you? You knew that she was Silver Dove ever since this all started!" Shadow fluffs out her feathers in annoyance, as if she is insulted by my question. When she speaks, her usually gentle voice is full of venom.

"Of course I knew, I am the guardian of the medals. I would be a very bad guardian if I didn't even know who has them. I've known since the moment she first put on her medal. Her grandmother gave it to her, just as your uncle gave it to you. She was the Silver Dove before Colomba and her grandfather was the Crow before you!" My body begins to shake with rage as fire seems to flow through my veins. I glare at Shadow in silence for a moment, unsure of what to say to her. I have always thought of Shadow as a friend, and sometimes she has also acted as a mother to me, but right now all I can see her as is an enemy, the one who betrayed me. After everything we have gone through together, how could she keep this from me?

"You knew how I feel about Colomba, yet you still let me fight her and cause her so much pain?!

You let me become her enemy?!" Shadow's feathery little body fluffs up even more for a second, enraged by my words, before she takes off into the air so that she can fly right in front of my face, her beak only an inch from my nose. Her black eyes stare right into mine as her stern voice scolds me.

"I had to do that to make sure things were right!! Do you think you were worthy of that information at the time?!" Her voice is cold, instantly killing the fire I felt inside. Now all I feel is guilt at her words. Her tone makes me want to hang my head in shame, but I keep looking at her, wanting to see what she has to say. "You were using your powers for your own goals, trying to make her like you, but you were not worthy of your powers, let alone her at that time. You were a broken little child then, wanting to lash out at the world. You needed to learn to accept yourself before you could let anyone that closely into your life. You needed to learn to love yourself before you could love her. I thought that you were almost at that point when you said that you would stop with this stupid plan of yours, but then you went right back to it. And now you plan on trying to drag her into your plan?! Are you crazy?!" I look down, not wanting to look into her furious dark eyes when I say what I think. I practically whisper it, feeling saddened by what Shadow has just said to me.

"You said that I needed to love myself before I could love her, but I've always loved her Shadow. I thought you would have seen that." I feel her wing swat my face, almost like she is trying to slap me without hands.

"What you had was not real love at that time! It was unhealthy! You cared for her, you loved her, but you could not love yourself then! You cannot truly love and be in a healthy relationship with a person until you can love yourself! Until you love yourself, all you can have is a little crush or a toxic love! Loving someone without loving yourself will always end in pain." I sit down at my desk, trying to get away from her, but she follows and perches herself on a mug holding my pens and pencils. Her voice is a bit more gentle now, but she is still scolding me like a parent scolding their kid for breaking something. "You always told yourself that you couldn't be worthy of her because of who you are, but you were wrong. She cares about you despite what everyone thinks. Colomba has shown how much she cares about you millions of times, but you were so stuck on your own misery to even notice. I kept that secret from you so that you could have a chance to learn and so that you could grow more and so that she could be safe from you." Her last sentence immediately starts another fire in me.

"Safe from me?!" I roar in my fury. *"And what do you mean by that?!"* Shadow doesn't even flinch at my rage.

"Yes, safe from you. Think of all the things you have done with your powers. Do you think she would have been safe being around you considering how most people feel about you?" Her question actually makes me stop to think. Would she have been safe around me if I had still done a lot of the same stuff as the Crow? People would have seen her as a villain too and they might have done something to her. Or, a thought that hurts me deep in my soul, back then if she had still tried to fight back against me even though we knew who each other were, I may have done something to hurt her even though I love her. I may have tried to fight her to try and win. Would I have really done that? I want to say that I wouldn't, but with how I have acted out of emotion before, I don't know how truthful that is. Shadow is right, I could have been the monster in that situation. Colomba did need to be protected from me. I bury my face in my hands.

"Oh my gosh, you're right Shadow. I'm sorry." I look down at my sketchbook on my desk where all my sketches of my past soldiers have been drawn. Just looking at that book makes the fire start to catch inside of me again. "But I need to try, I need to try one last time." Without giving her a chance to fight with me again, I place my hand over the Crow Medal and she disappears into it.

I feel bad about making her disappear like that, but I need silence right now. I need to think. I have some important things I need to do tomorrow. I'm going to talk to Colomba about this, about everything. We need to figure this out together so that we know how to move forward. My mind is already swirling, trying to figure out what I will do, and what I can say to her to try and get her to join my side. I know it will take a lot to convince her, but I know that it will be worth it. I need to have her by my side, I am willing to do almost anything to make sure that happens. I just know that I can't hurt her, I would bend over backwards for her if she merely asked, I couldn't do anything against her.

I will figure something out, I know it. For now though, it's getting late. I start getting ready for bed, it's a little early to go to sleep, but I have a big day ahead of me tomorrow and I want to be fully rested for what is to come. So many things are about to change tomorrow, I can feel it. Whether or not it will be what I want, or what Silver Dove wants, that I don't know, I will have to see how things turn out tomorrow.

Chapter Fifteen
Colomba-
The Next Day

All around me, people are excited, the dance will be happening tonight, but I can't share their excitement. I am too terrified to even think about having fun. My eyes are scanning the crowd around me as we all enter the school to start the day. I'm praying to find some sign of the Crow or something. I'm still hoping that I somehow got myself home last night, but I have serious doubts about it. The Crow was probably the one that did it, and that thought just absolutely terrifies me. I was so worried about it that I barely slept last night, I'm probably running on about three hours of sleep right now. As I hear people chatting with their friends, I'm surprised by how few people are talking about what happened yesterday with me and the Crow. I have only heard a few people talk about it, but they are all only talking about this one part of it, the part where I told everyone about how I hate being Silver Dove. They are all shocked that I said that since they all think it would be great to be a superhero, but they all avoid the part where I called them all out for never helping and pretty much causing all of these problems. They all probably feel a bit too uncomfortable to discuss that, because they know it's true. Nobody wants to talk about their sins, they keep that locked in their own hearts.

Nat is talking to me, but I am barely listening. I feel a bit bad about that, but I do have a lot going on in my mind right now. If she knew what is really going on in my life I think she would understand. From the corner of my eye, I notice something that immediately takes my mind out of my thoughts and back to reality. Kaley is rushing towards Nat and I, I feel myself stiffen with worry before I see her smiling face and I know that she doesn't mean us any harm. Kaley starts walking with the two of us, and I notice that her smile is a little nervous.

"Hi Nat." Kaley says, her voice quivering a bit in her fear. Nat looks at her curiously, obviously seeing that something is up.

"Hey Kaley, what's up?" Kaley looks at her feet, afraid to look at Nat and I in the face.

"Well, I know that the dance is tonight, so I'm a bit late asking you this, but do you think we could go together- you know, like as a date?" My eyes grow wide in shock as I finally understand what has been happening with Kaley these past few days. She wasn't getting made fun of just because she likes someone, she was getting made fun of because she liked another girl. It feels like someone has just stabbed me in the heart, and no one is around to help me stop the bleeding.

Looking over to Nat, I can tell that she's

holding back an excited smile. She clears her throat awkwardly before she answers Kaley.

"Yeah, I would like that a lot." Kaley's face lights up with pure joy as her cheeks turns bright red in her embarrassment and delight.

"Great- that's really great." Kaley stutters out. "I guess I'll meet you here tonight then." Nat looks down at her feet, trying to hide the giant smile on her face.

"Yeah, yeah I'd like that a lot." The two of them are both awkwardly looking at their feet for a moment before Kaley starts backing away from us.

"I'll see you tonight then, bye." And without another word, Kaley wanders through the crowd, trying to desperately get away from us as fast as she can. As soon as she is gone, I turn to look at Nat with a huge smile on my face. Nat looks over at me from the corner of her eye, embarrassment coming over her face.

"What?" Nat asks quietly, her eyes darting from her feet and then back to me.

"That was the cutest thing I have ever seen in my entire life." Nat toys with her braids as she looks away from me in her awkwardness.

"Shut up." She starts walking away from me, but I follow her with a little skip in my step.

"How can I shut up when I've just witnessed the cutest thing that has ever happened on this planet?" Nat keeps messing with her braids, the usual sign that she's nervous or embarrassed.

"You mean… you're not mad at me, or you don't want to be my friend anymore?" I look at her, trying to figure out what on earth she's talking about.

"What do you mean Nat?" We both stop walking to look at each other, the conversation suddenly becoming very serious.

"Well, I thought that if anyone found out that I like girls too, then they wouldn't want to be around me anymore." I let out a soft sigh, feeling almost disappointed in Nat.

"And you thought that I would abandon you too, despite everything we have gone through together?" Nat suddenly looks very ashamed of herself.

"I shouldn't have thought that, you are my best friend and we have gone through a lot together. I was just so afraid Colomba, I didn't want to lose my friends." I hold her in a tight embrace, hoping I can squeeze out her fears with a good hug.

"You never have to be afraid of losing me, I'll always be here for you Nat." I clear my throat awkwardly, if she has revealed that to me, then I guess now is a good time to reveal something to her. "Nat, I should tell you this too, you're not alone with this. I'm actually asexual, I don't really have any attraction to anyone." Nat gently moves out of my hug, holding me out at arm's length so that she can get a clear look at my face to see that I'm not lying. I smile sadly at her. "I guess I was afraid of the same thing as you." The two of us smile at each other, not saying a word. Nothing really needs to be said. We understand and care about each other, no matter what may change, that's all that needs to be understood.

The beautiful moment we are sharing gets

broken as we hear a girl screaming in terror, and then more people start screaming with her. We look around to see terrified people looking up, and when we follow their gaze, my blood freezes in my veins at what I see. The Crow is flying over the crowd trying to get into the school. He isn't doing anything, just flying above us like he is waiting for something. When the screaming dies down, he yells down to us like he is our ruler trying to order us around.

"Silver Dove! Come to me now, we need to talk!" What on earth would that crazy weirdo want to talk to me about? I don't have time to think about that though; I need to get all these people to safety, transform into Silver Dove, and then see what this idiot wants. I shout to the silent crowd around me.

"Everyone, run inside and get to safety!" Nobody argues with me, they all charge into the school like a stampede. Within the chaos, I let myself lose Nat in the crowd so that as soon as I get inside I can slip inside a janitor's closet without anybody noticing in the confusion. It only takes a second for me to transform, but I wait an extra second or two for the sounds of people running to stop before I leave the room and head back outside to find out what the Crow has to say to me. I am afraid of what is to come, but I don't let that fear control me, I have people I need to protect. I am the hero, and this is what I am meant to do, whether I like it or not.

Chapter Sixteen
Luis-
All is Revealed

After all the students get inside, it doesn't take long for Silver Dove to fly out the front doors of the school, her sword held tightly in her hand, like she is prepared for a fight. I don't fly away from her though, I could never be afraid of Colomba, even if she is still believes that I am a monster that she needs to slay. She stops right in front of me, seeing that I am not moving to do anything to her, she can tell that I just want to talk, so she is kind enough to not attack me. A girl like her would never hurt anybody who isn't trying to hurt her. I can see her perfect eyes glaring at me from behind the helmet she wears. It hurts to see so much anger directed at me from those beautiful, gentle eyes. A heavy silence hangs between us as we both fly in one place, just staring at each other, almost daring each other to break the silence. Apparently, Colomba is a lot braver than I am (not surprising to me), since she breaks the silence.

"What do you want Crow?" I open my

mouth to try and say something to her, anything, but nothing comes out. I close it again, feeling more awkward than I have ever felt in my life. Colomba just holds her head high waiting for me to say something, but when nothing comes out of my mouth her patience dies. "C'mon, you called me here for a reason, now what is it?" I take in a deep breath, knowing that I may frighten her with what I am about to say.

"I know who you really are now, Colomba." As soon as I say her name, the confidence she was showing moments ago fades completely to be replaced by terror. She is so shocked that she even stops flapping her wings for a moment, she started flapping them again as soon as she started to fall slightly. "I saw you change back to your normal self yesterday after our fight. I am so sorry Colomba, I never wanted it to be you." I take another deep breath to try and hold back the tears that are threatening to fall down my face. "To think of all the things I have done to you, the girl I have loved for so long, without even knowing it. It sickens me to think about. If I could go back in time, I would change everything so that we could have worked together from the very beginning. It doesn't mean that it's too late though." I reach out and hold her hand, she is too shocked by the fact that I'm doing this to pull her hand away, and I use this to my advantage. "I'm sure you know by now that those who wear the pins are destined to be together, so we should use our powers to help each other, to complete our goals. I want you to fight alongside me so that we can stop all the pain here, and then we can rule over them to make sure that it doesn't happen again." Colomba shakes her head sadly at me as she gently pulls her hand out of my grip. She looks up at me, like she is pitying me, I hate it.

"You know I won't do that Crow, I could never hurt anybody. And you know that this plan of yours wouldn't be for the best. You can't change people by force, they need to change of their own free will. We can only live our lives the best we can, and let them either learn their lesson or deal with the consequences, but I won't be the one giving out the punishments." I lower my head, not wanting to look at her, not wanting to see the pity and defiance in her eyes. Why can't she see this? Why can't she see that I am right? I feel my heart racing as anger starts to rise in me.

"Some people won't change though! People need to have someone above them who will make them act the right way!" She looks at me as if I am a toddler having a tantrum.

"And who are we to tell them what's right and wrong?" Her voice is soft and careful, yet also scolding me. I am instantly reminded of Shadow with how she is speaking to me.

"We are the ones with power! We could have them doing what we want, and make sure that nobody is in pain again! They are too stupid to realize how bad they are, they need guidance! And I will do everything in power to make them learn, and give the people they have made suffer get the power they deserve after everything they have gone through!" Colomba only looks at me, a deep sadness in her eyes, like she is looking at me and seeing a dark future. She sees me as just an obstacle in her life that she will always have to deal with. She lets out a faint sigh before she speaks.

"If that is how you truly feel, then I will keep fighting you until the day we die, because I will never use what gifts I have to harm anyone. They have hurt me in the past, but that doesn't mean I will take it out on them. People make mistakes, and we should learn from them. You need to either learn from your mistakes now and change, or I will give you the consequences of your actions." I knew she would say something like that, I didn't have much hope that she would change her answer, but I had to still try at least one time. Taking in a deep breath, to try and gain some courage, I look back up to her to tell her what I should have years ago. When I speak to her this time, I don't use the deep, strong voice I always use as the Crow. I let that die away so that I use my normal, quiet, scared, pathetic little voice.

"Colomba, it's me, Luis." Her eyes grow wide behind the mask, as if she can't believe what she just heard.

"Luis? Is it really you?" Her voice is just barely above a whisper, and I have to strain myself to hear it over the flapping of our wings.

"Yes, yes it's me." She shakes her head, and I can see tears building in her eyes.

"But, why would you do this? Why would you cause so much pain for everyone?" When I hear that question, the pain inside me leaves and I am filled with nothing else but rage.

"*Why?! Why?!* It's because of all of them!" I

point down at the school as if it is the most disgusting, hateful thing on the planet. "All those people in there cause so much pain every day. Ever since I was a kid, they treated me like I was nothing until I started believing I was nothing! They would push me down every day, beat me up whenever they could until I would be afraid to come to school, and they would do their best to make me miserable every single day. The teachers saw this every day and they didn't bother to do anything because they didn't care and that would take too much effort for them to bother… and then I met you." I look right into her eyes, seeing everything I could ever want in those eyes. "You were the only person who treated me- well, like a person. Everything started getting better for me when I met you, but things were still so bad for me, and for so many others. I needed to do something, because nobody else was going to." I turn my gaze away from hers, too afraid to see her perfect eyes looking at me anymore. "They ruined so much of my life, I didn't want to have that happen forever, and I didn't want it to happen to anybody else." Colomba flies closer to me, until we are only a foot apart. Slowly and carefully, she takes my hands in hers. I look into her eyes to see all of the love and affection she feels towards me reflected in her gaze.

"They have your past, but you have your future. Just because some bad things happened in the past doesn't mean that you have no future. You said that things were getting better for you, keep working to make that into the life you want. Don't let them win by letting yourself stay miserable. You are the only one responsible for your emotions." I look into her perfect eyes, and I know that she is right, but I don't want to believe it. I don't want to believe that I let this happen in my life, that I let myself be miserable when I had someone like her in my life; when I've had people like Nat, my uncle, and Mr. Sizemore looking out for me. I let this happen. All the emotions I have been holding in since yesterday when I found out who she really is starts pouring out, and tears flow from underneath my mask. I bury my face in my hands, filled with too much regret to even be able to describe it, like I have been lost my entire life and even though I've been found I am still lost in my new world.

"What have I done with my life?!" It's hard to breathe through all the sobbing, but I still manage to speak, letting out everything I've felt for so long. "I've hurt so many people! I didn't mean for all this to happen! I just thought that if I did this then everyone would change, that nobody would have to be afraid anymore! I failed! I failed so many people! So many of them were hoping that I would win, and I failed them! I failed myself and I failed you! You went through so much because of me! I caused you so much pain!" As I say that, my heart seems to shatter even more than before, which I didn't think was possible. Knowing that I have caused her so much pain is the worst thing I have felt. "What have I done with my life?!" To my surprise, I feel someone gently wrapping their arms around me in a soft embrace. I lift my head from my hands to see that Colomba is hugging me, trying to comfort me despite everything I have done.

"It's okay Luis, I'm here. You were being human, you made mistakes. That doesn't mean that you can't change. This isn't game over for you, this is just a new chapter." I begin to sob again as I hug her back, holding her tightly. I know what she means by what she said.

It means we can still be friends, that doesn't have to change for us. It means that we will finally start working together as the Crow and Silver Dove. It means that I am forgiven, and that is the greatest gift I could have ever gotten, a gift I don't really deserve. We hold each other tightly, knowing that this may be difficult to get used to, but it will be worth it, if we can still be friends after this. I know that the entire school is watching us, and they are all probably freaking out that we are hugging right now, but I don't care. All I care about is that I am here holding Silver Dove, holding my perfect Colomba.

Chapter Seventeen
Colomba-
What Happens Next

As soon as we release each other from our hug, we look deeply into each other's eyes and seem to just know what we need to do without having to say a word. The two of us fly over to the window of the school with the most people at it. I can already see countless phones pointed at us, recording everything that is happening. Everyone trying to understand what is going on in all the chaos. When I am flying in front of the window, holding the Crow's hand, I see countless phone camera flashing, trying to capture this strange event. I hold up my hand and everyone falls quiet at my silent command, they can all see that I am about to say something very important.

"Everyone, there is no reason to be afraid anymore. The Crow has told me who he really is and that he is giving up on his goal. He is willing to join my side and do what is necessary to make things right in this world. Everything is going to be alright now." The cheering from inside the school is deafening. I can hear the windows vibrating from all the noise, it is that loud.

Looking over at the Crow, my best friend Luis, I can see how uncomfortable and afraid he is right now, seeing all these people cheering for him. I squeeze his hand gently, and he lets his gaze leave the crowd to look back at me. The fear in his eyes melts when he looks into my eyes. A gentle smile comes over his face, and nothing more is needed to be said, he understands what I mean. I will protect you. I won't let them hurt you. You made your mistakes, and now it is time to prove to the world that you have changed. I will be with you the entire time, looking out for you.

While the school still cheers for us, the two of us fly off to somewhere nobody will see us, and we transform back into our usual selves. It is simple then to slip into the school and join everyone else to start the first class of the day. Sadly, I had to separate from Luis at that point so he could go to class, but he is stronger than he thinks, he can survive without me for a little while.

My first class passes by quickly, and I get to rejoin Luis in second period. By this point, people are starting to show each other clips from the news, showing what happened this morning between the two of us. The newscasters are a little skeptical to believe that the Crow has really turned over a new leaf, but they are optimistic. Luis, once again, got super uncomfortable hearing people doubting him, but a simple hug was the only thing needed to help him feel better.

The rest of the day passed just like that, the

only thing anybody could talk about was what happened with me and Luis. Thankfully, the two of us survived the day without anything else happening. I still can't believe what happened myself, to think I have been fighting my best friend all this time and we didn't realize it until now. I feel like an idiot for not realizing it sooner. I mean, I have suspected him before, but something happened that made me think he was innocent again. I can't remember what it was now.

My heart breaks as I think of all the things that he said this morning. Has he really been in all this pain for so long? I knew he got picked on a lot, and I tried to help him whenever I could, but has there been a lot more to it than I thought? I feel like I have really let down my friend, but there was no way I could have known. He never told me, and I tried to help whenever I saw something happen, I can't really blame myself for stuff I didn't see or hear about. If I know that, then why do I still feel guilty?

Another feeling is overpowering my feeling of guilt though, and I don't know exactly what it is. He had said that he has been miserable and in pain for a long time, but he also told me that he loves me. The Crow has told me that multiple times over the years, so I know that I didn't mishear him earlier. Does he really mean that? Does he actually love me or is this just a little crush? Nonna did say that those who wear the pins are destined to fall in love, and Luis seems to know that somehow too. Did he just start thinking that he needs to be in love with me because of that, or has he always felt this way? I don't know how to feel, I don't know what I should do. Should I do anything about this or go on pretending like he never told me? I mean, he has always been a good friend to me, and I have thought before about how he would be a good boyfriend to someone, but I never thought he would be interested in me, so I never let myself think like that. Do I love him too, or do I view him as just a friend?

These questions run through my mind all day, and before I know it the school day is over, and I am back at my house getting ready for the junior prom. I slip into my dress and get down the stairs just as Luis arrives with his uncle to pick me up. We get into the car, ready to have a wonderful night, despite how confused and weird we both probably feel. We chat with his uncle the entire way there and arrive without any issues. Only when we are alone in front of the school do we both fall silent, unsure of what to say or do.

"A lot… a lot has happened today, hasn't it?" I ask awkwardly, just trying to break the silence. Luis just smiles down at me, looking rather handsome in his black suit. He can obviously tell how awkward I feel, but he doesn't make fun of me for it.

"Yeah, yeah there has, but I think it was all good things. I'm glad with how things turned out. We've got a lot to talk to each other about, and I have so much I need to show you. Plus, I need to introduce you to Shadow." I narrow my eyes in confusion, but he just smiles at me. "Don't worry I'll explain later, for now, let's just have a good time." He holds out his hand to me, which I happily accept, and he leads me through the gym doors to enter the prom.

Chapter Eighteen
Luis-
Junior Prom

As soon as we open the doors, we are greeted by pounding music and bright lights shining in the dark room. All around us people are dancing, chatting, and eating snacks. Everyone is having a good time, and so am I. Honestly, I can't believe how lucky I am right now. Even after everything I have done, Colomba has forgiven me, we will be working together, and here I am side by side with her at this dance. She looks so beautiful right now.

Her lovely dark hair falls past her bare shoulders, while a beautiful white dress covers her. She has a white shawl, that she definitely made herself, draping over her shoulders that looks as delicate as a spider's web. Her gentle, aquamarine eyes look at me with joy and without saying a word, we walk to the dance floor together and dance to a slow and gentle song. Neither of us speak as we dance along with everyone else, we don't need to, we understand how happy we both are. This is probably the happiest I have ever felt in my entire life. When I was planning everything the other day before I found out who she is, I never expected this would be how things turn out. Here I am dancing with the girl of my dreams, knowing that she has been fighting me for years as Silver Dove, yet we are both happy. We have forgiven each other, and we are eager to start things over between us. I may not be going after the goal I've been chasing for years now, but I believe I am on a better path now. I have Colomba by my side, any side with her is the best one.

Once the song is over, we both drift over to a table where Nat and Kaley are sitting together, eagerly chatting and holding hands. I smile softly when I see this, I'm so glad that they were able to be together for this, they look so happy just being with each other.

After I grab a drink for Colomba and I, I sit down beside Colomba, the two of us joining in the conversation Kaley and Nat were having. Just like everyone else today, they are talking about what happened between Colomba and I did as Siver Dove and the Crow.

"I don't know about you guys," Kaley says cautiously, "but I don't know if the Crow is going to keep their word and start working with Silver Dove. I don't know if someone can change that fast." I instantly feel awkward hearing this since I know that so many other people probably feel the same way. That misery disappears as I feel Colomba's hand rest on mine. I look up to see her smiling comfortingly at me before she says.

"Well, I think he's telling the truth. You've got to have faith in people to make the right decision." I smile back at her, knowing that she believes in me. What did I do to deserve having someone like her in my life? Nat chuckles at what Colomba said.

"There's our Birdy, always the optimist." We all gently laugh at the teasing. I can't help but feel optimistic too, things are going to be better now. I can feel it. We are all about to start chatting again when an unpleasant thing interrupts us.

"You look beautiful tonight Colomba." None of us are very surprised when we see Alex standing beside Colomba's chair, smiling down at her while completely ignoring everyone else at the table. Colomba smiles at him politely, but without any enthusiasm.

"Thank you, Alex." She starts to turn so that she can continue talking to me, but he keeps talking.

"This is a pretty nice dance, isn't it?" I can see Colomba roll her eyes a bit before she responds.

"Yes, it is." He grins at her mischievously.

"Well then why aren't you dancing?" He takes her hand, and without any explanation, he takes her out to the dancefloor where they are playing a fast song that everyone is dancing wildly to. As soon as they are on the dancefloor, Alex starts dancing like a madman while Colomba looks at him awkwardly for a moment. It's obvious that she doesn't want to be there, but she starts dancing with him, probably just trying to be polite again. I watch them with anger flowing through my veins as I watch them dance together, sometimes I wish she wasn't so polite. I wish that she would just tell him to leave her alone like I know she wants him to. As I think this, the fast song ends to be replaced by a much slower song. Many of the people leave the dancefloor, while the rest begin to slow dance. I watch in horror as Colomba tries to walk back over to where we are sitting, but Alex pulls her in close. He smiles down at her with trouble in his eyes. My entire body tenses with rage at the sight of it. Beside me, I can hear Kaley and Nat stop talking, they have noticed this too and they seem to be just as worried as I am.

"C'mon Colomba." I can hear him saying faintly over the quiet music. He sounds as if he is trying to be romantic, his voice sound and persuasive. "We've been teasing each other for long enough, kiss me, I know you want to." Once again, he doesn't give her a chance to respond before he starts leaning in close to her face so he can steal a kiss from her. Colomba uses both of her hands to push against his chest, trying to get out of his grip. Colomba may be strong for her size, but I don't know anybody who can beat Alex in a test of strength. My blood instantly begins to boil in my veins at what I'm seeing. I bolt out of my chair, seeing red as my eyes never leave Alex. I can hear Kaley and Nat try to tell me to come back, that I'll get myself killed doing this, but I don't care. Nothing matters to me except her, I won't let him hurt her. I rush over to them as fast as I can without any thought of what might happen to me. I push Alex back as hard as I can, which isn't much, but with Colomba and I pushing at the same time, it at least makes Alex stumble backward a step or two and he releases Colomba from his grip. Alex stares at me with shock for a moment before his expression instantly changes to fury.

"What do you think you're doing, freak?" His voice is full of fury, but right now, he could never match the ferocity I feel after seeing what he was trying to do. My hands clench into fists at my side as I glare at him with all the hatred I have ever felt towards him.

"What am I doing!? What are you doing!? What were you trying to do to her!?" Alex's eyes grow wide. He has never heard me sound this angry and strong before, I don't think *I've* ever heard myself sound like this before either. "It's obvious that she doesn't want to talk with you, she doesn't want you around! You are always trying to force her attention on you even though it's clear to everyone that she doesn't like it! She is just trying to be polite to you, even though you don't deserve it! You are annoying and pathetic! You make fun of others so that you can feel better about your own miserable life!" I move closer to him so I can whisper my final message, so Colomba won't hear me. "And I'm not afraid of you anymore."

Alex's face is a mask of shock and misery from my words. The mask seems to get ripped off in a second though to be replaced with fury. It looks like he is about to either scream or hit me, until he looks back at Colomba. I don't dare to let my eyes leave him to look back at her, but from his expression he is very upset by what he sees. When he looks at her, the anger leaves him, and he looks like he is about to cry. Without another word, he walks away, his head hanging low, as if he has finally realized that he is the monster here.

Only when he is far from us, do I turn back to face Colomba, to see if she's alright. She is staring at me with wide eyed shock, obviously surprised that I actually stood up to Alex. Honestly, I'm kinda surprised with myself too.

Her shock breaks into an emotion that I can't see before she wraps her arms around me in a warm embrace, her face buried in my chest. I wrap my arms around her as she thanks me in a soft, shaky voice. Glancing down at her, I am suddenly very concerned. It's only now that I notice that she is shivering against me, but it's not cold in here. She has her head lowered, so I gently use my fingers to lift her chin so I can look her in the eyes, her crying eyes. The sudden reality hits me, she wasn't angry or annoyed when Alex was doing all that to her, she was terrified. I hold her tightly as she buries her face into my chest again as she starts to sob. I gently stroke her hair, trying to soothe her.

When I glance up, I notice something that makes my eyes narrow in confusion. A lot of people around us have stopped dancing to stare at us with a mixture of pity and misery in their eyes. I notice that some of the people staring at us like that shift their gaze over to Alex, and their emotions quickly change into fury and hatred.

It doesn't take me long to realize what's going on. They saw what Alex was trying to do and they are enraged. Colomba is very well known in this school for being very kind. Alex may be popular, but everyone knows that he's a jerk. After what they just saw him do, I don't think that even Alex's reputation can be restored no matter how rich his family is or how good he is at sports. He has shown his true colors, and nobody can forget that.

Alex seems to feel the hatred people are feeling towards him right now since he looks around to see dozens of people glaring at him. In his eyes, I can see his confusion at seeing their hatred, but when he looks back at me holding Colomba tightly as she cries, he seems to figure it out. Without another word, Alex leaves the gym without even looking at his group of friends who are all hanging out together by the door. Even they glare at him a bit as he passes by them as well. Something in my gut tells me that things are going to be a whole lot different in this school after tonight. For now though, I have something far more important that I need to focus on.

Looking down at Colomba, she still has her face buried against my chest as I feel her body shaking with sobs while I hold her tightly. My heart feels like it is getting ripped out of my chest and torn apart seeing her like this. I need to say something, I need to make her feel better. I could never just let her suffer like this.

"Colomba, you don't have to worry about Alex anymore, he just left so he won't bother you again tonight. And I will always be here to make sure he never bothers you again. I don't care what he does to me, he has already hurt me countless times, so I don't care anymore. I won't let him hurt you." She holds onto me even tighter, as if she is afraid that I will leave her in her time of need, but I would never do that to her. Over the pounding music, I can only faintly hear what she says with her face buried against my shirt.

"I was just so scared. He is always so pushy with me, no matter how many times I told him I'm not interested. He scares me so much sometimes. Why can't he just leave me alone?" I gently stroke her hair like how my uncle used to do it to comfort me when I was little.

"He will leave you alone, I'll make sure of it. I won't let anything bad happen to you, ever." She lifts her head from my chest, her perfect aquamarine eyes still filled with tears, while a grateful smile is on her lips.

"Thank you Luis." The slow song continues to play and all around us on the dance floor are couples swaying in time to the music together. Colomba rests her head against my chest, no longer burying her face in my shirt as she sobs. Now she just rests it there as we start to sway to the music with everyone else. With her so close to me, I can feel her crying begin to die down as she relaxes against me, completely at peace once again. I want to kiss her, I want to do that so badly. This seems like such a romantic time to have a first kiss. I mean I finally stood up to Alex, I defended her from him, and a beautiful slow song is playing that we are dancing to together.

To most this would be the perfect time, but when I look down at her, I know that it would be all wrong. I mean, I defended her against Alex because he was trying to force a kiss on her, it would probably feel like a betrayal if I tried to kiss her right now after that happened. I can wait, I can be patient. Now is not the right time to try and make a move. Right now is a time to comfort her. I have defended her from him and finally joined her side as the Crow. We've made a lot of steps forward together today, I don't want to overwhelm her by doing that too. I want her to be comfortable with me, after all the stuff I have done as the Crow, I will probably need to rebuild a lot of trust with her, but I'm willing to do that. I'm willing to do anything to have her in my life. As Silver Dove and the Crow, we are meant to be together, so I know that I have time to prove my love and have her accept that love. We have all the time in the world, and I'm just happy that we can spend that time together.

We spend the rest of the dance together, happily spending time with each other; dancing, talking, and hanging out with friends. It was a perfect night. I was disappointed when it was time for it to end and my uncle came to pick us up. Now I am in my room, getting out of my suit while Shadow looks at me with joy in her eyes. It doesn't take long for her to explain why she is so happy with me.

"You have done so much today that I am so very proud of Luis." I smile down at her as she perches on my bed.

"Thanks Shadow. I'm sorry it took me so long to figure everything out. You were right all along, and I should have listened. I'm so sorry." Shadow chuckles softly, shaking her head at me.

"Not too long after we met, I told you that it was impossible to not make mistakes, but it takes a truly amazing human being who can admit their mistakes and try to fix them. I believe that you have finally become that amazing human being I always thought you were." I smile at Shadow, feeling so happy that she is proud of me. For the first time in ages, she is proud of me. I know that I have been a big disappointment to her for years, it feels so good to know that I am no longer causing her pain.

"Thank you, I will do whatever it takes to make sure that you are always proud of me. I won't disappoint you again." The two of us just look at each other. I know that birds can't smile, but I can tell that Shadow is very happy with him.

A faint tapping on my window makes the both of us look over and I smile with joy. Flying right outside my window is Colomba as Silver Dove, waving at us with a playful grin on her face. I go over to open the window so that she can ask me a question.

"Hey want to come out flying with me; it's a beautiful night for it?" Without even thinking, I nod my head, always eager to spend more time with her. I turn to Shadow, and I don't even need to say anything for her to understand. She takes off from the bed and flies around me, faster and faster, until I have become the Crow.

I have to struggle a bit to get my large wings out the window, but when I do, the two of us are immediately flying through the air, feeling the crisp night air blow on our faces and through the feathers of our wings. We fly over the town and into the countryside, soaring over barns and endless farmland. The rest of the world seems so far away with the two of us here flying through the clouds.

I look over at Colomba, feeling so much joy

because I know that my life is now changing for the better. For the first time in a long time, I feel hope for the future because I know I will have her by my side. If I have her then I know that things will be fine. With her, I know that my life will get better. I have become the better person I was meant to be, and I have a person by my side who will stick with me through thick and thin. No matter what happens, we will get through it because we will do it together.

Neither of us need to say anything, it seems like we both just know what the other is thinking. We fly high above the world, ready to start this new chapter in our lives together. I'm ready to face it all with her.

Chapter Nineteen
Colomba-
The Dream

Curling up under my covers, I let out a deep sigh of relief. I just got back from my late night flight with Luis, and I still can't believe how great everything is right now. It feels like the weight of the world is off of me for the first time in years, ever since I got the pin and became Silver Dove. I finally have someone to help me with my journey as Silver Dove, I am not alone anymore. I feel as if I have been fighting against the world for so long, but now I have someone who will join the battle with me. In the past few days I have found out who the Crow is, I've had them finally stop fighting me, they are joining my side, and I may even have Alex off my back now. It all feels so wonderful, and kinda unbelievable after everything I have been dealing with since I became Silver Dove. It seems that all my big problems in life have just disappeared in the last few days, and it's all thanks to Luis. With him turning over a new leaf, I don't have to worry about the Crow anymore, and I have someone to help me keep the world safe, and he even stood up to Alex for me. And from the way Alex looked earlier tonight, I'm guessing he won't be messing with me again. Luis really is so wonderful. I am so lucky that I have him by my side.

I smile to myself as I bury myself deep into my covers while my thoughts trail off as I think about memories of Luis, and wonder about the future we will have fighting side by side. We won't have to focus on fighting each other, now we can focus completely on making the world a better place and doing whatever we can to help those in need. We will be doing our purpose as Silver Dove and the Crow, we will be creating peace, and I am so happy that Luis finally sees it that way too. Those happy thoughts lead me into a pleasant sleep. The darkness of sleep does not last long before I open my eyes to a familiar dream.

I am a little dove, flying through the air and I land in the courtyard of the same building I always land in within this dream. Just like every time I have had this dream; it goes through the exact same thing. I am in the courtyard with the fountain with the three figures on top of it, each person having some kind of bird with them. I notice the crow underneath the willow, and I fly through the swaying branches of the willow to reach it. The two of us embrace and enjoy each other's company until the crow gets scared by something flying above us. The crow tries to shield me from whatever it is, but it crashes through the branches and swats the crow out of the way to get to me. With my tiny dove body, it holds me in one clawed hand as it says something to me in a deep, menacing voice, "I will be coming for you soon, my love. I am almost out of here, just wait for me."

I don't know what this creature means by that, but it moves closer to me as if it is trying to kiss me, but the sunlight breaks through, hitting this shadowy creature, letting it erupt in a bright golden light. The creature lets out a piercing cry as I squirm out of its grip to see this creature completely engulfed in the light. I try to look through the light, to try and finally figure out what this thing is, but I only see the figure of a human- like creature with what looks like angel wings in the light. I try to get closer, but whatever this is, it's blinding me, keeping me back.

The strange creature lets out another earsplitting shriek, and something clicks in my mind, it sounds almost… familiar. It sounds like the cry of a bird, a very large bird. I look toward the fountain at the final figure on it. The one of a young man with the largest bird on their shoulder. I squint my eyes to look closer at it. I see it!! I know what it is after all these years!!! And I think I know what it means!!! It's a-!!!

My alarm clock blares, waking me up. I groan a little as I rub the sleep from my eyes. As I look out my window to see the rising sun, I try to remember what my big discovery was in my dream. No matter how hard I try though, I can't remember what I had discovered. I know it was important though, I remember feeling so happy and excited about figuring it out. Why is it that as soon as you wake up, you can't remember stuff about your dreams? It is so frustrating.

I let out a little sigh as I kick my blankets off of me so that I can start getting ready for the day. It was just a dream, it's not like it was something super important, so I shouldn't let myself get upset by it. I have a lot that I need to do today, so I can't let myself get distracted. As I get dressed, I think about what needs to get done today. Since it is the weekend, I have a lot of chores and such to do around the house, but since I told Nonna about how Luis is the Crow, she might be willing to let me get out of it for once so that I can hang out with him and discuss things with him. We do have a lot to talk about. I'll need to text him later to try and figure out when we can meet up to talk. I can only wonder what he will tell me about in regards to his powers and all the stuff he has gone through because of it.

While everything is peaceful in my home though, something is happening in the woods outside of town. Within a dark patch of trees, something is arriving, a dark memory of the past, but not my past. That thing that is arriving, is going to cause this now peaceful time to become another war. If I only I knew, maybe I could have stopped all the pain I will be feeling in the future. I couldn't know that though, I had no way of knowing. I would just have to continue on with my day, not knowing the horror I would be experiencing. Not knowing that my world will soon begin to fall apart.

Don't miss the previous books in The Adventures of Silver Dove series. Check them out at elizascalia.com.

Eliza Scalia is a therapist who has a master's degree in Clinical Mental Health from Troy University. She enjoys reading, writing, and needlework. Eliza has been writing since she was in middle school and has self- published the Death's Assistant series for young adults. She lives with her husband Paul and her dog Lady.